THE THREE MUSKETEERS

BY PETER RABY

ADAPTED FROM ALEXANDRE DUMAS' NOVEL

**DRAMATISTS
PLAY SERVICE
INC.**

SPECIAL NOTE

Anyone receiving permission to produce THE THREE MUSKETEERS is required to give credit to the Author as sole and exclusive Author of the Play on the title page of all programs distributed in connection with performances of the Play and in all instances in which the title of the Play appears for purposes of advertising, publicizing or otherwise exploiting the Play and/or a production thereof. The name of the Author must appear on a separate line, in which no other name appears, immediately beneath the title and in size of type equal to 50% of the size of the largest, most prominent letter used for the title of the Play. No person, firm, or entity may receive credit larger or more prominent than that accorded the Author.

THE THREE MUSKETEERS was first presented by the Stratford Festival in Ontario, Canada, during the season of 1968. It was directed by John Hirsch; the designer was Desmond Heeley; and the music was by Raymond Pannell. The cast, in order of appearance, was as follows:

D'ARTAGNAN'S FATHER	....	Kenneth Pogue
D'ARTAGNAN	....	Douglas Rain
D'ARTAGNAN'S MOTHER	....	Joyce Campion
HIS NURSE	....	Nancy Kerr
FAMILY PRIEST	....	Peter Scupham
INNKEEPER OF THE JOLLY MILLER	....	Eric Donkin
INNKEEPER'S WIFE	....	Jane Casson
ROCHEFORT, the Cardinal's agent	....	Malcolm Armstrong

BICARAT	Officers of the Cardinals Guards	Jérome Tiberghien
JUSSAC		Patrick Crean

MILADY DE WINTER	....	Martha Henry
MME. COQUENARD, in love with Porthos	....	Barbara Bryne
BONACIEUX, a grocer, Husband of Constance	....	Bernard Behrens
COQUENARD, Husband of Mme. Coquenard	....	Adrian Pecknold
M. DE TREVILLE, Commander of the King's Musketeers	....	Max Helpmann

PORTHOS	Musketeers, the "Three Inseparables"	James Blendick
ARAMIS		Christopher Newton
ATHOS		Powys Thomas

MME. DE CHEVREUSE, in love with Aramis	....	Nancy Kerr
KITTY, Milady's maid	....	Anne Anglin
CONSTANCE, Wife of Bonacieux, lady-in-waiting to the Queen	....	Mia Anderson
THE DUKE OF BUCKINGHAM	....	Kenneth Pogue
LOUIS XIII, KING OF FRANCE	....	Eric Donkin
ANNE OF AUSTRIA, Queen of France	....	Pat Galloway
LAPORTE, the Queen's valet	....	Kenneth Welsh
DONA ESTEFANIA, lady-in-waiting to the Queen, the Cardinal's informant	....	Joyce Campion
GRIMAUD, servant to Athos	....	Northern Calloway
PLANCHET, servant to D'Artagnan	....	Robin Marshall
CARDINAL RICHELIEU	....	Leo Ciceri
GERMAIN, a Palace Guard	....	John Turner

INNKEEPER AT CHANTILLY .... Peter Scupham

TWO STRANGERS } .... { Leon Pownall
Christopher Bernau

LANDLADY OF THE GILDED LILY .... Barbara Bryne
A SEA CAPTAIN .... Max Helpmann
LE COMTE DE WARDES .... Christopher Bernau
PATRICK, servant to Buckingham .... Louis Thompson
MR. O'REILLY, Buckingham's jeweller .... Bernard Behrens
LANDLADY AT CRÈVECOEUR .... Jane Casson
A JESUIT .... Eric Donkin
A CURÉ .... Adrian Pecknold
LORD DE WINTER, brother-in-law to Milady .... Kenneth Welsh

ENGLISH LORDS } .... { David Foster
Terry Judd
Leon Pownall

BRISEMONT, a bandit .... Leon Pownall
ANOTHER BANDIT .... Lawrence Benedict
INNKEEPER AT THE RED DOVECOT .... Bernard Behrens

SOLDIERS } .... { Guy Bannerman
Christopher Bernau
Lawrence Benedict

FELTON, a Puritan .... Christopher Walken
AN ENGLISH GUARD .... Terry Judd
ABBESS OF THE CONVENT AT BÉTHUNE .... Nancy Kerr
EXECUTIONER .... Kenneth Pogue

Musketeers	Cardinal's Guards
Lawrence Benedict	Guy Bannerman
Christopher Bernau	Terry Judd
Robin Marshall	Neil Munro
Leon Pownall	Leon Pownall
Christopher Walken	Louis Thompson

OTHER CHARACTERS PLAYED BY .... David Daiken, Ian Gaskell, Ken Gibbings, Pamela Gruen, Danny James, Tedde Moore, Ken Scott, Jim Wyatt

A MUSICIAN .... Robert Comber

4

LIST OF SCENES AND CHARACTERS

(These are minimal requirements—some of the fight sequences could use more.)

ACT ONE

SCENE 1. Outside the D'Artagnan home: Béarn, Gascony.
D'Artagnan; his father, his mother.

2. The Jolly Miller: Meung, on the road to Paris.
Rochefort; Jussac; Bicarat; D'Artagnan; Innkeeper; Milady.

3. A street: Paris.
Rochefort; Jussac; Bicarat; Milady; Bonacieux; Mme. Coquenard; D'Artagnan; Coquenard; (passers-by).

4. M. de Tréville's Headquarters.
Musketeers; Sergeant; Porthos; Aramis; D'Artagnan; M. de Tréville; Athos; Rochefort; cloaked figure.

5. Behind the Luxembourg.
Athos; D'Artagnan; Aramis; Porthos; Jussac; Bicarat; 3 Guards; Mme. Coquenard; Coquenard; (passers-by).

6. M. de Tréville's.
King; de Tréville; D'Artagnan; Athos; Porthos; Aramis.

7. The Louvre.
Constance; Buckingham; Laporte; Queen; Dona Estefania.

8. D'Artagnan's apartment.
D'Artagnan; Aramis; Athos; Grimaud; Porthos; Planchet; Bonacieux; Bicarat; 2 Guards.

9. Richelieu's Palace.
Cardinal; Dona Estefania; Bicarat; Rochefort; Bonacieux; Milady.

10. Bonacieux's shop.
D'Artagnan; Planchet; Bicarat; 2 Guards; Constance; Bonacieux.

11. The Louvre.
King; Cardinal; Jussac; Queen; Laporte; Dona Estefania; Guard.

5

12. Bonacieux's shop.
    Bonacieux; Constance; D'Artagnan; Athos; Aramis; Porthos; Planchet.

13. Shoulder of Mutton: Chantilly.
    Stranger; Innkeeper; Porthos; D'Artagnan; Aramis; Athos; Porthos.

14. A bridge near Crèvecoeur.
    2 Workmen; D'Artagnan; Aramis; Athos; Grimaud; Planchet.

15. Gilded Lily: Amiens.
    Athos; D'Artagnan; Planchet; Grimaud; Landlady; 2 Guards.

16. Windsor Castle.
    Buckingham; Milady.

17. The Harbour: Calais.
    Sea-Captain; Comte de Wardes; D'Artagnan; Planchet; Milady.

18. Buckingham's Palace.
    D'Artagnan; Patrick; Buckingham; O'Reilly.

19. The Louvre.
    Cardinal; Jussac; Bicarat; Milady; Rochefort; King; Guards; Queen; Constance; Dona Estefania; Laporte; D'Artagnan; (lords and ladies).

ACT TWO

SCENE 20. London and Paris: the Start of a Campaign.
Buckingham; Patrick; Cardinal; Rochefort; de Tréville;
D'Artagnan; Jussac; Planchet.

21. Shoulder of Mutton: Chantilly.
Porthos; D'Artagnan.

22. Black Lion: Crèvecoeur.
Planchet; D'Artagnan; Aramis; Jesuit; Curé.

23. Gilded Lily: Amiens.
Landlady; de Winter; Ormsby; D'Artagnan; Planchet;
Athos; Grimaud.

24. Milady's Apartment.
Milady; de Winter; Kitty; D'Artagnan.

25. A Paris Church.
Porthos; Mme. Coquenard.

26. Milady's Apartment.
Milady; Kitty; D'Artagnan.

27. An exchange of letters.
Aramis; Beggar; Athos; D'Artagnan; Kitty; Milady.

28. The Coquenards' House.
Mme. Coquenard; Porthos; Apprentice.

29. Milady's Apartment.
Milady; D'Artagnan; Kitty.

30. Outside the Louvre.
King; Cardinal; Queen; de Tréville; Athos; Porthos; Aramis;
D'Artagnan; Rochefort; Guards; Bicarat; Jussac; Milady;
Bandits; Kitty; Mme. Coquenard; Musketeers; (passers-by).

31. Outside the walls of La Rochelle.
Cardinal; Rochefort; Jussac; D'Artagnan.

32. Outside La Rochelle: on patrol, and D'Artagnan's tent.
D'Artagnan; Bandits; Planchet; Athos; Aramis; Porthos;
Grimaud.

7

33. **Red Dovecot.**
3 drunk soldiers; Innkeeper; Porthos; Aramis; Athos; Cardinal; Jussac; Rochefort; Milady.

34. **D'Artagnan's tent.**
D'Artagnan; Porthos; Aramis; Athos; Planchet.

35. **Lord de Winter's Castle near Portsmouth.**
Planchet; de Winter; Milady; Guard; Felton.

36. **The Louvre.**
Queen; Laporte.

37. **Lord de Winter's Castle.**
Milady; Felton; Guard; de Winter.

38. **Portsmouth: Buckingham's Flagship.**
Patrick; Buckingham; Felton; Guard; de Winter; Laporte.

39. **The Convent: Béthune.**
Abbess; Milady; Constance; Rochefort; D'Artagnan; Athos; Porthos; Aramis; de Winter.

40. **The Riverbank.**
Milady; Planchet; Grimaud; Athos; Porthos; Aramis; D'Artagnan; Executioner; de Winter.

41. **Paris.**
Cardinal; Jussac; D'Artagnan; Rochefort; Athos; Porthos; Aramis.

A NOTE FROM THE ADAPTOR
AND THE DIRECTOR

violence, love, money, politics

Dumas' novel rests on four basic ingredients of violence, love, money and politics. He wrote it in instalments for a daily newspaper, and when the paper's circulation faltered, he whipped up the mixture. The historical romance was one of the earliest pop entertainments for mass consumption, a forerunner of the Western and the comic strip, and Dumas' Romanticism has none of the wispy pallor of the Pre-Raphaelites, but the vivid golds and reds of Delacroix, the primary colours of Lichenstein. It's fairy-tale, and Arthurian legend-time. The figures are archetypes—D'Artagnan is related on one side to Lancelot, on the other to Don Quixote, Athos to the Cid (and Humphrey Bogart), Milady to Morgan Le Fay (and Marlene Dietrich). It's also dream-time: money flows into D'Artagnan's hands, women fling themselves at him, his actions affect the fate of nations. And nightmare-time: the dream, like many romantic fantasies, turns sour, just as the gay free-thinking students waving banners for liberty are transformed into a mob hurling stones and battered by truncheons—just as Robert Kennedy stares out from the cover of Time Magazine, the emblem of half a nation's hope, to be mown down by an asassin's bullet. Today the world seems to be in the throes of a Romantic movement not unlike that of Dumas' Europe after the upheavals of the French Revolution and the Napoleonic era. Bludgeoned by war and news of war, paralysed by bureaucracy, many are seeking through clothes, drugs, sexual freedom and entertainment a more primitive and innocent world. In this adaptation and production, we have tried to instill from Dumas' sprawling extravaganza the highly-coloured essence of a persistent and still potent Romanticism.

John Hirsch
Peter Raby

The Three Musketeers

ACT ONE

SCENE 1

Outside the D'Artagnan home: Béarn.
A neigh. A Monday evening in spring, very early. It's cold.
D'Artagnan's parents stand outside their house.

FATHER. My son, I'd hoped to see you leave home better mounted. (*A neigh.*) Charlemagne's older than you. But he served me well in two wars, and he won't let you down. Here's a purse with fifteen crowns: not very much, but enough to get you to Paris. This is a letter to Monsieur de Tréville, my oldest friend—and your Godfather. It was thirty years ago that he and I set out from Gascony to make our fortunes, and now he's captain of the King's Musketeers. He has great influence with his Majesty. Look on him as a father and listen to his advice. Finally, here's my sword.

D'ARTAGNAN. I can't take that, father.

FATHER. Take it. My fighting days are over. I'm sure you'll be worthy of it. I've taught you everything I know. Above all, remember you're a D'Artagnan, and a Gascon.

D'ARTAGNAN. Yes, father.

FATHER. There are only three men in Paris you need respect: The King, the Cardinal and de Tréville. For all the rest, you are their equal. A man is known in this world not by his possessions but by his courage. So fight on every possible occasion; and fight all the more readily because duelling is forbidden. Your mother's got something for you.

MOTHER. It's a recipe an old gypsy woman sold me—for a wonderful ointment. She said it would heal every wound that doesn't pierce the heart.

D'ARTAGNAN. Thanks, mother. I may need it.

MOTHER. Goodbye, my dearest. Write to us sometimes.

D'ARTAGNAN. Goodbye, mother. Goodbye, father.

FATHER. Goodbye, my boy; and God's blessing on you. (*D'Artagnan leaves. Sound of horse hooves. His parents stand waving.*)

SCENE 2

The Courtyard of the Jolly Miller.
The Comte De Rochefort, Jussac and Bicarat. They are drinking wine.

ROCHEFORT. Jussac—Bicarat—tell me if you can see what I see. Is that an orange horse lumbering into the yard?

JUSSAC. It's certainly orange—but is it a horse?

D'ARTAGNAN. (*Off.*) Whoa there, Charlemagne.

ROCHEFORT. The reincarnation of Rosinante. And here is Don Quixote himself, fresh off the farm, with the muck on his boots still steaming. (*D'Artagnan enters.*)

D'ARTAGNAN. (*Over his shoulder.*) Groom, look after my horse.

ROCHEFORT. He thinks it's a horse. (*Bicarat and Jussac laugh. Rochefort allows himself a faint smile.*)

D'ARTAGNAN. Look here, sir. You there, sir.

ROCHEFORT. Can he be talking to me?

D'ARTAGNAN. Yes, you sir. Tell me what you find so amusing. Perhaps I can share the joke. (*Rochefort walks past D'Artagnan to get a better view.*)

ROCHEFORT. It is an astounding color—for a horse.

JUSSAC. Perhaps he started life as a buttercup.

ROCHEFORT. Quite a common shade for a flower, of course, but unknown in horses—until today.

D'ARTAGNAN. Sir, we treat that horse like one of the family. So when you insult him, you're insulting me.

ROCHEFORT. As you may guess from my appearance, I don't often indulge myself by laughing. But I insist on laughing when I please.

D'ARTAGNAN. And nobody laughs when it displeases me. (*He draws his sword.*)

ROCHEFORT. Indeed? Well, no doubt you were cock on your own dungheap. You'll find the world has other standards.

D'ARTAGNAN. A man is known in my world by his courage. So turn and face me, if you don't want a thrust in the back.

ROCHEFORT. The peasant's more bovine than he looks. (*D'Artagnan lunges at him, and Rochefort has to draw. His men take over with fire-tongs and shovels.*) Guards! (*D'Artagnan is finally overpowered.*) Another damned Gascon. Stick him on his orange horse and send him away.

D'ARTAGNAN. Not before I kill you for that insult.

ROCHEFORT. These Gascons never learn. Keep up the tattoo then, if he hasn't had enough. Harder, boys, they've hides like oxen. (*D'Artagnan is beaten insensible. The Innkeeper, who has entered during the fight, attends to him.*) Bicarat, ask Milady to hurry. The Cardinal is inclined to be impatient.

BICARAT. Yes, Monsieur. (*Bicarat goes.*)

ROCHEFORT. How is our young hothead?

INNKEEPER. He's in no condition to give you any more trouble.

ROCHEFORT. I find nothing but trouble in your filthy establishment. Boorish guests and rancid wine. Where are those horses?

MILADY. (*Appearing above with Bicarat.*) I hear you were threatened by some insolent cub, Chevalier. Did you cover yourself in glory?

D'ARTAGNAN. (*Reviving.*) With shame, with shame. Now Monsieur, will you refuse my challenge in the presence of a lady?

MILADY. I should love to see you in action, Chevalier. But can we risk delay?

ROCHEFORT. Milady, you have an unrivalled sense of priority. Jussac, ride on ahead and make sure we have fresh horses at Versailles. (*Jussac goes.*) Nothing must distract us from our mission. We can still be in Paris by morning. (*Rochefort, Milady and Bicarat prepare to leave.*)

INNKEEPER. Monsieur!

D'ARTAGNAN. Coward!

INNKEEPER. What about my bill? (*Finds the crowns in D'Artagnan's pockets.*) Still, this one's got some money, and we should have him on our hands for a few days.

D'ARTAGNAN. Swindler! (*Bicarat throws some money to the Innkeeper.*) Who is that man?

INNKEEPER. I'd forget about him if I were you, sir. What you need is a comfortable bed, good food and wine . . .

13

D'ARTAGNAN. Well, he's a coward, whoever he is. But she . . .
INNKEEPER. Milady?
D'ARTAGNAN. Milady . . . is so beautiful. (*He faints.*)

SCENE 3

M. Bonacieux is on his way home from market. Madame Coquenard is doing her shopping. Rochefort arrives with Milady, Jussac, Bicarat and Guards.

ROCHEFORT. Jussac, Bicarat, you may leave us here. We shall go straight to the Cardinal's Palace. (*They leave.*)
MME. COQUENARD. How much are those onions?
BONACIEUX. Twenty centimes the bunch.
MME. COQUENARD. What would I do with a bunch of onions? I'll take the two smallest. And you can throw that tomato in for nothing—it's rotten, you'll never sell it. (*D'Artagnan enters with M. Coquenard.*)
COQUENARD. Three crowns—you're a lucky young man.
D'ARTAGNAN. You'll look after Charlemagne. He's almost a friend.
COQUENARD. We're very partial to horses in our family. My dear, I trust you haven't been extravagant. At least we've no need to visit the butcher for some time. (*He and his wife go.*)
BONACIEUX. You look like a new arrival.
D'ARTAGNAN. My first hour in Paris. I'm looking for somewhere to stay.
BONACIEUX. I think I can help you there. My name's Bonacieux: I've a lovely room over my shop in the Rue des Fossoyeurs—a stone's throw from the Luxembourg. Only ten crowns a week, payable in advance.
D'ARTAGNAN. I'll take it. Perhaps you'd carry my bags—I have an appointment with M. de Treville. I expect to be made a Musketeer.
BONACIEUX. Their headquarters are that way. Au revoir—Musketeer! (*They leave in opposite directions.*)

14

De Tréville's Headquarters.
Musketeers erupt onto the stage. They swirl their cloaks
twirl their mustaches, laugh heartily, and sing:

MUSKETEERS.
  *Each morning early
  We're on parade
  Forsaking mistress
  Abandoning maid
  Straight from a drunken night of
  Wine, dice and cards
  Straight from the Louvre where
  We mounted guard:
  O we are the King's most gallant Musketeers
  We have no equals and we have no peers
  The women all surrender, the enemy despairs
  When faced with the King's Musketeers.
(*The Sergeant drills the Musketeers.*)
SERGEANT-MAJOR Mousquetaires, rouges et noirs.
MUSKETEERS. Oui.

SERGEANT-MAJOR. Êtes-vous prêts?
MUSKETEERS. Oui, monsieur.

SERGEANT-MAJOR. Allez, un, deux, trois, quatre. Tirez l'épées.
Un, deux, trois. En garde. Chapeaux; salute. En garde. Avancez.
Balestre, un, deux. Les ripostes. Rompez en arrière. Gardez en
retraites. Un, deux, trois. Rompez, jouez messieurs. (*The Sergeant-
Major leaves. The Musketeers embark on an informal workout.
D'Artagnan has entered during the drill.*)

D'ARTAGNAN. Excuse me, Monsieur. I have a letter of introduction to M. de Tréville.

1ST. MUSKETEER. Your name?

D'ARTAGNAN. D'Artagnan. (*Musketeer goes.*)

PORTHOS. Musketeers!

2ND. MUSKETEER. When isn't Mme. D'Aiguillon the King's
subject?

*The Play Service cannot provide music for this song. The Adaptor
suggests that it be sung to the melody of a traditional marching song.

3RD. MUSKETEER. At night, when she's under the Cardinal. (*Laughter.*)

D'ARTAGNAN. Things have changed since my father's day.

ARAMIS. (*Trying to complete a poem amongst the sword-play.*)
Flowers in springtime bloom around her bed,
Oh, heart must follow where the heart is led.

3RD. MUSKETEER. When will Aramis become a priest?

4TH. MUSKETEER. When the Queen's produced an heir. (*Laughter.*)

PORTHOS. Then he'll have to wait till the Duke of Buckingham breaks down her resistance. (*Laughter. He fends off an opponent.*) Touché.

1ST. MUSKETEER. (*Returning.*) M. de Tréville will see M. D'Artagnan. Musketeers! Salute. (*The Musketeers salute de Tréville.*)

DE TRÉVILLE. (*Entering.*) Porthos! Aramis! Athos!

1ST. MUSKETEER. Rompez! (*All leave, except Porthos, Aramis and D'Artagnan, who remains with some embarrassment.*)

DE TRÉVILLE. Gentlemen, let me tell you what the King said to me today. "From now on," he said, "I shall have to recruit my Musketeers from the Cardinal's guards."

PORTHOS. What the devil did he mean by that?

DE TRÉVILLE. He meant that the Musketeers have water in their veins. They need some fresh red blood. The Cardinal entertained the Court yesterday with an amusing story. It seems a gang of drunken Musketeers were brawling in a bar, and a patrol of his Guards arrested them. Musketeers arrested! I've never been so humiliated. And you three were there—the Cardinal named you. It's my fault. I suppose— Aramis, why in the devil's name did I ever give you a uniform? You're only fit to wear a cassock. Porthos, damn your vain eyes, you're nothing but a walking clotheshanger. And Athos—where is Athos?

ARAMIS. He's dangerously ill, sir.

DE TRÉVILLE. What's wrong with him?

PORTHOS. The doctor's afraid it's measles.

DE TRÉVILLE. At his age? You mean he's wounded, God blast you. That's the last straw. Musketeers arrested, one of my best men wounded, and the Cardinal's crew don't have a scratch to show for

16

it. I shall offer my resignation to the King. (*Athos appears, pale but upright.*)

ATHOS. I was informed that you had sent for me, sir. I'm at your service. Have you any orders?

DE TRÉVILLE. Athos, my brave friend, I was about to forbid my Musketeers to risk their lives needlessly. Because I know, and the King knows, that they're the salt of the earth. Your hand, Athos. (*Athos' wound is in his right shoulder, de Tréville's handclasp makes him faint.*) A surgeon. Mine—the King's—the best. (*Porthos and Aramis carry Athos inside. A surgeon scurries across.*) Too bloody proud to admit he's wounded. My brave Athos. Curse, the lot of you. (D'*Artagnan draws attention to himself.*)

D'ARTAGNAN. M. de Tréville.

DE TRÉVILLE. What! Oh, young D'Artagnan. You must excuse me. An officer has to look after his men. How's your good father? And what can I do for his son? Haven't seen you since your christening.

D'ARTAGNAN. Sir, I've always dreamed of wearing a Musketeer's uniform.

DE TRÉVILLE. So does every Gascon worthy of the name. But the King hand-picks his men. I daresay I could stretch a point and make you a cadet—that will give you a chance to distinguish yourself. Would that do?

D'ARTAGNAN. Whatever you suggest, sir.

DE TRÉVILLE. I'll see to it right away. My boy: you'll find Paris a bit different to Gascony. The Cardinal's word is law here, and the law forbids duelling. So take my advice: keep your head out of politics, your hand out of duels, and your heart out of love. (*Rochefort crosses, giving de Tréville a curt greeting.*)

ROCHEFORT. Monsieur.

D'ARTAGNAN. Sir—who is that man?

DE TRÉVILLE. That's the Comte de Rochefort, the Cardinal's agent: Keep out of his way, he's a dangerous customer. Be warned, D'Artagnan. (*He leaves.*)

D'ARTAGNAN. Well, he insulted me, and he'll pay for it. (*Athos enters. D'Artagnan crashes against his shoulder as he runs out.*) I'm sorry—I'm in rather a hurry.

ATHOS. You think that's sufficient reason to cannon into me? You need an elementary lesson in etiquette.

17

D'ARTAGNAN. And where do you propose to instruct me?
ATHOS. Behind the Luxembourg—at noon. (*Athos goes off.*
D'Artagnan continues after Rochefort as Porthos emerges. This
time, D'Artagnan becomes enveloped in Porthos' cloak and tears
it off.)
PORTHOS. Do you run with your eyes shut, you blinkered
yokel? I think you've earned a thrashing.
D'ARTAGNAN. Behind the Luxembourg?
PORTHOS. Agreed. At one o'clock.
D'ARTAGNAN. At one.
PORTHOS. At one. (*Porthos moves off. D'Artagnan runs out.*
Aramis enters with two Musketeers.)
1ST. MUSKETEER. How does that poem of yours begin, Aramis?
ARAMIS. Oh, it's nothing, nothing at all.
2ND. MUSKETEER. We thought it was charming. Do recite it.
ARAMIS. Did you really? Well, if you insist.
"Flowers in springtime bloom around her bed
    To screen perfection from the curious eye.
    Oh, heart must follow where the heart is led."
It's a villanelle, you know.
1ST. MUSKETEER. A villanelle?
2ND. MUSKETEER. We'd never have guessed. (*A cloaked figure*
passes, and discreetly lets fall a handkerchief. Aramis puts his foot
on it.)
ARAMIS.
    "And man must grasp what woman cares to shed
    To shield her name from gross profanity:
    Flowers in springtime bloom around her bed."
The next line escapes me. It will come back. (*D'Artagnan has re-*
turned.)
D'ARTAGNAN. What a beginning! I've offended M. de Tréville
by ignoring his advice, and now I've fallen out with two of his
Musketeers. I must acquire more finesse. Perhaps I can model my-
self on Aramis.
1ST. MUSKETEER. My dear Aramis.
D'ARTAGNAN. Good morning, gentlemen.
ALL. Good morning. (*They take no further notice.*)
D'ARTAGNAN. I believe this is your handkerchief? (*Aramis*

makes frantic efforts to keep his foot on it, but D'Artagnan retrieves it and is presenting it to him when the 1st Musketeer snatches it.)
1ST. MUSKETEER. What a divine scent. Madame d'Aiguillon? No—too much musk.
2ND. MUSKETEER. A suspicion of ambergris—Madame de Chevreuse.
1ST. MUSKETEER. Venetian lace.
2ND. MUSKETEER. Such delicate embroidery.
ARAMIS. The gentleman's made a mistake. I have my handkerchief here.
1ST. MUSKETEER. You're blushing, Aramis. Flowers in springtime bloom around her bed.
2ND. MUSKETEER. And what else follows where the heart is led?
1ST. MUSKETEER. It's a villanelle, you know.
2ND. MUSKETEER. A villanelle? *(They go.)*
ARAMIS. That was a most ungallant action. People do not tread on handkerchiefs without a reason. The streets of Paris are not paved with lace. You have forced me to compromise a lady's reputation.
D'ARTAGNAN. You shouldn't conduct your love affairs in public.
ARAMIS. Monsieur. I see you have just arrived from the Provinces. You will find me behind the Luxembourg at one.
D'ARTAGNAN. I've another appointment at one—at two?
ARAMIS. At two. *(Aramis bows and goes.)*
D'ARTAGNAN. Bring both your handkerchiefs, you may need them. *(He leaves.)*

SCENE 5

Behind the Luxembourg.
The twelve strokes of noon. Athos is waiting, making a few passes with his rapier. D'Artagnan arrives, breathless.

ATHOS. You're very punctual, Monsieur. I'm afraid my friends are late.
D'ARTAGNAN. I haven't got any seconds. The only man I know in Paris is my godfather, M. de Tréville.
ATHOS. Then he'll think me a child-murderer.
D'ARTAGNAN. Hardly, Monsieur, when you have the disadvantage of such a serious wound.

ATHOS. I'll use my left hand. Don't imagine I'm making things easy for you. I happen to be ambidextrous. In fact, you'll find a left-handed opponent decidedly awkward. My apologies for not warning you. Still, you made my shoulder burn.

D'ARTAGNAN. You're most courteous, Monsieur. I have a wonderful ointment, which I'm sure would cure you in three days. And then I'd be honoured to keep our engagement.

ATHOS. Monsieur, I admire your spirit. If I don't kill you, we can look forward to a pleasant acquaintance. But I can't accept your offer. We live in the days of the Cardinal, not Charlemagne; if we postponed our duel for three days, the secret would be all over Paris. Besides, here's the first of my friends. (*Aramis enters.*)

D'ARTAGNAN. M. Aramis!

ATHOS. Have you any objections? (*Porthos appears.*)

D'ARTAGNAN. M. Porthos!

ATHOS. Naturally. We are called the Three Inseparables.

PORTHOS. What's he doing here?

ATHOS. This is the gentleman I'm going to fight.

PORTHOS. But so am I.

D'ARTAGNAN. Not until one.

ARAMIS. I have an appointment with him myself.

D'ARTAGNAN. But not until two. Gentlemen, allow me to offer you an apology. (*The three begin to sneer.*) You misunderstand me. I'm simply apologizing in case I can't fulfill all my obligations. M. Athos has the right to kill me first, which makes your challenge far less interesting, M. Porthos, and yours, M. Aramis, practically worthless. And now . . . (*Beginning to strip off his jacket.*) . . I'm ready.

ATHOS. It is hot. But I shan't remove my jacket, as my wound's begun to bleed again; and I shouldn't like to taunt you with the sight of blood you haven't drawn.

D'ARTAGNAN. You're most considerate. (*He replaces his jacket.*)

ARAMIS. Etes vous prêts, Messieurs?

D'ARTAGNAN & ATHOS. Oui.

ARAMIS. En garde, allez! (*They begin to fight.*)

PORTHOS. The Cardinal's guards. (*Jussac appears with Bicarat and three Cardinal's Guards.*)

JUSSAC. Musketeers! You know the law against duelling. Sheathe your swords, and come with me.

ARAMIS. M. Jussac, we should be delighted to accept your invitation, but sadly we must decline. M. de Tréville has issued the most rigorous instructions.

JUSSAC. Then we'll take you by force.

ATHOS. (*Forming a group with Aramis and Porthos.*) Five against three, and I'm wounded. Still, better to die than appear in disgrace again before our Commander.

D'ARTAGNAN. Gentlemen, you said you were three. But I make it four.

PORTHOS. You're not one of us.

D'ARTAGNAN. I may not wear the uniform, but I have a Musketeer's heart. On my honour if we're defeated I shan't be alive to see it.

ATHOS. What's your name, my friend?

D'ARTAGNAN. D'Artagnan.

ATHOS. Well then, Athos, Porthos, Aramis and D'Artagnan—on guard! (*They fight.*)

D'ARTAGNAN. Behind you, Jussac.

ATHOS. Don't kill him, D'Artagnan. I've an old quarrel to settle with him when my wound's healed. (*By the end of the fight, all of the Guards are dead or disabled, except Bicarat.*)

JUSSAC. (*From the ground.*) Surrender, Bicarat—

BICARAT. A Bicarat never surrenders.

JUSSAC. That's an order.

BICARAT. Oh, if it's an order, that's different. (*He breaks his sword over his knee, throws the bits away, then crosses his arms and whistles.*)

JUSSAC. We'll have our revenge. (*Jussac and Bicarat leave.*)

D'ARTAGNAN. And now, gentlemen, I'm ready for you.

PORTHOS. I think honour's been satisfied.

ARAMIS. If you fight for us, you can't fight against us.

ATHOS. D'Artagnan, we appoint you: Honorary Musketeer!

ALL. All for one, and one for all! (*Passers-by appear.*)

SONG: "ALL FOR ONE AND ONE FOR ALL"*

All for one and one for all
All for one and one for all

*The Play Service cannot provide music for this song. The Adaptor suggests that it be sung to the melody of a traditional marching song, such as, "Men of Harlech".

21

With fame our reward
And death in our sword
We'll shed our blood for France.
MME. COQUENARD. You remember my cousin, M. Porthos.
PORTHOS. M. Coquenard, Mme. Coquenard. (*She slips Porthos a note.*)
M. COQUENARD. Who are these noisy people?
MME. COQUENARD. They're Musketeers, my dear.
SONG:
We are the King's loyal Musketeers
With our support he has no fears
We duel and sing
And die for our King
To serve la belle France.

All for one and one for all
All for one and one for all
With fame our reward
And death in our sword
We'll shed our blood for France.
(Exeunt)

SCENE 6

De Tréville's.
The King calls on de Tréville.

DE TRÉVILLE. Your Majesty.
LOUIS. A little bird told me the news, Tréville—I couldn't resist dropping in to congratulate you. This more than makes up for yesterday—the Cardinal will be mortified. (*The four enter and salute the King.*)
DE TRÉVILLE. Musketeers!
LOUIS. Athos—Porthos—Aramis—and you must be the cadet who sliced up Jussac. What's your name?
D'ARTAGNAN. D'Artagnan, Your Majesty.
LOUIS. You're a brave man. You're all brave men. I'm proud of you. Can't approve officially, of course. And when it comes to a war, I'll expect you to bury the hatchet. But as long as you choose

a quiet corner, your Commander and I will look the other way. (*He puts a bag of gold in D'Artagnan's hands.*)

D'ARTAGNAN. Your Majesty.

LOUIS. Tréville, I think I'll take a glass of your madeira. I feel ten years younger. (*He leaves with Tréville.*)

D'ARTAGNAN. How shall I ever spend all this?

ARAMIS. Oh, that won't last long in Paris. Plan for the future and find a rich mistress.

PORTHOS. First things first, my dear fellow. Hire yourself a servant to look after your clothes.

ATHOS. There are only two essentials for tonight: a case of wine and a damn good meal.

D'ARTAGNAN. Gentlemen, I'm not very experienced in these matters. I'd be most grateful for your help. Would you consider joining me for dinner this evening?

ATHOS. All for one, then?

D'ARTAGNAN. (*Sharing out the money.*) And one for all. (*They go off.*)

SCENE 7

The Louvre.
Constance leads Buckingham in.

CONSTANCE. I don't think we were followed. Wait here, Your Grace. I'll bring the Queen. Monsieur Laporte, the Duke of Buckingham is here.

LAPORTE. Your Grace!

DUKE. I am pleased to see you, Laporte.

ESTEFANIA. Her Majesty, the Queen. (*The Queen enters with Constance and Estefania, who remain in the background.*)

QUEEN. You must have learnt by now that I never wrote the letter that brought you to Paris.

DUKE. I have, Anne. It was foolish to believe that marble could soften. But love isn't rational. And I've gained by the journey, because I have seen you.

QUEEN. At the risk of your life—Constance's life—my reputation. The only reason I'm seeing you is to tell you we must never meet again. It's sacrilege to struggle against the law of God.

23

DUKE. Isn't it sacrilege to separate two hearts God meant for each other?

QUEEN. I never said that I loved you.

DUKE. At least you've never denied it. You couldn't be quite so cruel to a love like mine. Anne, in three years this is only our fourth meeting. I've only once, for a few minutes, been alone with you. In the garden at Amiens . . .

QUEEN. Don't talk about that evening.

DUKE. You remember it? All the stars were out—the air was warm, and heavy with the scent of flowers. You held my arm as we walked along the avenues, and when you told me about the troubles of your life, you bent your head, and your hair brushed my cheek. Anne, I swear you loved me that evening.

QUEEN. Perhaps that evening . . . But let me remind you of the sequel. The Cardinal aroused the King's suspicions, my friends were exiled, and when you tried to return to France as Ambassador . . .

DUKE. The door was slammed in my face. But France will pay for her King's jealousy. If I can't see you, Anne, at least you'll hear of me every day. Why do you think I'm planning an expedition to relieve the Protestants at La Rochelle? The war will lead to a peace, the peace will require a negotiator, and I shall ride through Paris again—but this time as a conqueror. Thousands may die, but I'll see you again.

QUEEN. You mustn't do such things for my sake. I am Queen of France.

DUKE. And if you weren't the Queen, you would love me?

QUEEN. I didn't say that . . .

DUKE. If it's an illusion, let me live in it—perhaps die in it. I've had terrible dreams lately.

QUEEN. I had a dream last night—I saw you lying bleeding.

DUKE. With a knife in my left side?

QUEEN. How do you know? I've only told God in my prayers.

DUKE. Could God send us the same dreams unless we loved each other?

QUEEN. Leave me now. I can't tell whether I love you or not. I do know that I will never break my marriage vows. And that your love must not harm my country.

DUKE. I'd declare war on the whole continent for one glimpse of your face.

QUEEN. I'll give you something to remember me by. Take these diamonds. They're the most valuable jewels I have. They were given to me by the King on behalf of the people of France! While they're in your possession, let them be a pledge that you will keep peace between France and England. (*She gives them to the Duke. He kisses her hand.*) Constance.

DUKE. Marble to the end, Your Majesty. But I shall keep my word. (*Constance leads him out. The Queen goes in with Estefania.*)

Scene 8

D'Artagnan's apartment, above Bonacieux's shop. Aramis is reading his breviary and writing poetry. Athos is giving D'Artagnan a wine-tasting lesson. Athos' servant, Grimaud, is fishing for bottles and groceries.

ARAMIS. Poets must praise her now, while lovers sigh . . .

ATHOS. That, D'Artagnan, is claret. Château Latour. Not an especially good year, but a very sound wine. What have you found for us now, Grimaud? Ah, a Burgundy—Nuits St. Georges les Perdrix—a small vineyard but extremely consistent—the owner's an old friend of mine. First—the colour—then the nose. Now roll it round the palate. Slowly, slowly, savour the bouquet. We won't bother about spitting it out. Swallow it. Needs another year or two, but it has a certain modest charm. Excellent tactics, D'Artagnan, pitching camp over a grocer's.

D'ARTAGNAN. It was quite accidental.

ATHOS. Then you have the instincts of a true Musketeer, which is far more important. Aramis, you're not being very sociable

ARAMIS. Forgive me, D'Artagnan. My publisher's been pressing for poems and I'm two weeks behind with my prayers. (*He closes the breviary. Athos signals to Grimaud, who refills the glasses.*)

D'ARTAGNAN. Does Grimaud ever misunderstand you?

ATHOS. Very seldom: but I can always whip him; and when I'm

25

not in company, I value my silence. (*Porthos comes in, propelling Planchet.*)

PORTHOS. Sorry I'm late—had to keep a rendezvous with my chess. But I've found you a servant, D'Artagnan. His name's . . .

PLANCHET. Planchet.

PORTHOS. He was leaning over a bridge spitting in the water. That suggested a harmless, philosophical nature, so I engaged him on the spot. Thirty sous a day. He can press your suit for a start—and my tailor might manage to do something for it if Planchet takes it in tomorrow.

D'ARTAGNAN. Make yourself at home, Planchet. You can sleep under my bed.

PLANCHET. But I thought I was to serve this gentleman . . .

PORTHOS. What an absurd idea. Do I look like a man who has no servant? I shouldn't stand for any insolence of that sort, D'Artagnan.

D'ARTAGNAN. Planchet! (*He cuffs him.*) I forbid you to leave my service without permission. I know I'm going to be extremely successful, and I'm far too considerate a master to let you miss such a chance. (*He cuffs him again.*)

ARAMIS. Bravo, D'Artagnan.

PLANCHET. Much obliged, sir, very thoughtful, I'm sure.

ATHOS. And now, to dinner. Planchet, serve the pâté. Grimaud, baste those partridges.

PORTHOS. Pâté de foie gras—though I don't see any truffles. I'll have some of that garlic bread, Planchet.

ARAMIS. Foie gras is to cookery as the sonnet is to poetry. That, D'Artagnan, is a bon mot. The bon mot is a form you should master, D'Artagnan. It seasons one's conversation. You've read Montaigne, of course.

D'ARTAGNAN. Not a word.

ARAMIS. But he's from Gascony. My dear fellow, this is appalling. I shall have to take you in hand. Montaigne for thought; Ronsard for passion; and . . .

PORTHOS. Rabelais—for life.

ARAMIS. St. Augustine—for your soul. You'll find it essential to attend the right church. I myself hear mass at La Madeleine. Most of the best people go there, and all the elegant women.

ATHOS. Let Aramis advise you on literature, D'Artagnan—but

listen to me about women. Use them if you must, and then discard them. But keep out of their clutches. (*Bonacieux knocks.*)

D'ARTAGNAN. Planchet!

PLANCHET. Come in.

BONACIEUX. Good evening, M. D'Artagnan— Gentlemen. Sorry to disturb you at table.

D'ARTAGNAN. Haven't I seen you somewhere before?

BONACIEUX. This morning, sir. I own this house—my shop's on the ground floor, and you asked if you could take this apartment. Which reminds me, you never paid the rent.

ARAMIS. I shouldn't give him a sou, D'Artagnan, till he furnishes the place properly. It's not fit for a gentleman. No sign of a bookcase.

D'ARTAGNAN. Well, what do you want?

BONACIEUX. It's about my wife, sir. She's been abducted.

PORTHOS. Your wife?

BONACIEUX. She's only twenty—I married her last year, a miserable dowry they scraped together for her, but she's a pretty little thing: her godfather's the Queen's valet.

ARAMIS. M. Laporte?

BONACIEUX. That's right—and he got her a job at court as a lady-in-waiting. She's allowed home once a week, and tonight I went to meet her as I always do, you have to keep an eye on these young wives, and M. Laporte told me: abducted.

ATHOS. Did he know who by?

BONACIEUX. He suspected it was the Cardinal's agent. I saw him only this morning—a tall, dark man with a scar on his left temple.

D'ARTAGNAN. The Comte de Rochefort.

BONACIEUX. You know him?

D'ARTAGNAN. I've already sworn to kill him for insulting me. And now he's ravished your wife.

BONACIEUX. No, I prefer to believe his motives are political. My wife doesn't often let me into her confidence, but from hints she's let drop she's been employed as go-between in a love affair of . . .

PORTHOS. Madame d'Aiguillon!

ARAMIS. Madame de Chevreuse!

ATHOS. The Queen. (*Bonacieux nods.*)

D'ARTAGNAN. And?

BONACIEUX. Who else but . . .

ATHOS. The Duke of Buckingham.

BONACIEUX. I hurried home and there was this note in my shop. "Your wife will be returned when her usefulness is exhausted. If you value your life, don't attempt to look for her."

D'ARTAGNAN. That sounds serious. But it's only a threat.

BONACIEUX. I find threats like that very persuasive. Just a glimpse of the Bastille turns my stomach. But as you're connected with the Musketeers, I thought you might be interested in taking on the Cardinal's men. I'd forget about the rent.

D'ARTAGNAN. Are you rich?

BONACIEUX. I make ends meet, sir. Years of hard work and self-denial.

D'ARTAGNAN. Well?

BONACIEUX. Would fifty crowns interest you?

D'ARTAGNAN. That's more like it.

BONACIEUX. You'll consider it then?

D'ARTAGNAN. Fetch the money and we'll make a plan.

BONACIEUX. Oh, thank you, sir. (Bonacieux goes.)

ARAMIS. There is an air of mystery about this business which has its attractions. But is it worth risking our four heads for fifty crowns?

D'ARTAGNAN. A woman's in danger—a young, beautiful woman abducted, tortured perhaps—and all for serving her mistress faithfully.

ATHOS. D'Artagnan, woman was created for man's destruction.

PORTHOS. Besides, she's only a shopkeeper's wife.

D'ARTAGNAN. But she serves the Queen. Can we stand idly by while the Cardinal snuffs out all the Queen's friends?

ARAMIS. I wish she wasn't so enchanted by our enemies.

D'ARTAGNAN. Personally, I'd take the Duke of Buckingham by the hand and lead him to the Queen just to spite the Cardinal. He's our true enemy. (A clatter on the stairs and Bonacieux bursts in.)

BONACIEUX. Help, help, the Guards have come to arrest me. Help! (Porthos, Aramis rise and draw their swords. Athos remains seated. D'Artagnan motions them to sheathe.)

D'ARTAGNAN. Just a moment, Porthos. Let's use our heads.

PORTHOS. But you promised the old boy.

ATHOS. Let D'Artagnan decide. He's the most intelligent, and I'll go along with him. (*Bicarat and the Cardinal's Guards appear.*)

D'ARTAGNAN. Come in, gentlemen, come in. Welcome to my apartment. We're all loyal to the King and the Cardinal.

BICARAT. You won't prevent us carrying out the Cardinal's orders?

D'ARTAGNAN. On the contrary, we'll give you any assistance you need.

PORTHOS. Let's take a man each . . .

ATHOS. Keep quiet, you numbskull.

BONACIEUX. But you promised me . . .

D'ARTAGNAN. (*Aside to Bonacieux.*) We can only help you by staying free. If we take your side he'll arrest us too. (*To Bicarat.*) Here he is, gentlemen. He's been pestering me about my rent. Serves you right, you stingy old goat. A spell in the Bastille will teach you some respect.

BONACIEUX. But you promised me!

D'ARTAGNAN. Hang on to him as long as you can. M. Bicarat, a glass of wine?

BICARAT. With pleasure.

D'ARTAGNAN. Then we'll drink to your health.

ARAMIS. And to poor M. Jussac's.

D'ARTAGNAN. And to the King—and the Cardinal.

ALL. The King and the Cardinal.

BICARAT. Take him away. Much obliged for your assistance, gentlemen. (*He goes out with the Guards and Bonacieux.*)

PORTHOS. This is monstrous! Musketeers to sit here paralyzed while a poor old fellow who's been promised our help is dragged off by the Cardinal's henchmen.

ARAMIS. Porthos, Athos called you a numbskull and I agree with him. D'Artagnan, you're a great man.

PORTHOS. Well, I'm damned. Athos, do you approve of what D'Artagnan's done?

ATHOS. Naturally. I approve of it, and I congratulate him.

PORTHOS. I still don't follow.

ATHOS. Porthos, we used to be known as the Three Inseparables.

ARAMIS. And now we're four. So hold out your hands and swear.

ALL. All for one and one for all.

D'ARTAGNAN. Gentlemen, from this moment, we're at war with the Cardinal.

SCENE 9

Richelieu's Palace.
The Cardinal is completing an interview with Dona Estefania.

CARDINAL. So Mme. Bonacieux brought Buckingham to the Louvre.

ESTEFANIA. I know she did.

CARDINAL. And you're certain he took the diamonds with him?

ESTEFANIA. Certain, Your Eminence.

CARDINAL. Thank you for your help, Dona Estefania. You won't find me ungrateful.

ESTEFANIA. Your Eminence. *(He rings a bell. Bicarat comes in with a pigeon. Estefania goes.)*

BICARAT. Your Eminence. *(The Cardinal reads the message.)* Your Eminence, the Comte de Rochefort is here.

CARDINAL. Admit him. *(Bicarat beckons to Rochefort.)* The Innkeeper at Amiens tells me that Buckingham rode by at dawn heading for Calais.

ROCHEFORT. He can't be stopped.

CARDINAL. He should never have been allowed to leave Paris. But I know who can reach him in London. Do you have the Bonacieux?

ROCHEFORT. The husband's outside. The wife escaped.

CARDINAL. Rochefort, my patience is exhaustible.

ROCHEFORT. I'm sure Your Eminence's genius . . .

CARDINAL. Will cover up his agent's incompetence? I hope so, Rochefort, I hope so. There's a great deal at stake. That Queen's a perpetual menace to the safety of France. She'll beckon the Bourbons over the Pyrenees with one hand and Buckingham across the Channel with the other. Find out if she's written any letters today; and send in this Bonacieux creature.

ROCHEFORT. Bring in Bonacieux.

BICARAT. Bonacieux! (*Bonacieux edges into the room.*)

CARDINAL. And Rochefort—ask Milady to come and see me. (*Rochefort leaves.*)

BONACIEUX. Rochefort! That's the man who made off with my wife. No, no, Your Eminence, I'm quite wrong, no resemblance at all.

CARDINAL. Keep quiet. Bonacieux, the charge against you is treason. You've spent one night in the Bastille. Do you want to rot there?

BONACIEUX. It's nothing to do with me, Your Eminence. All I know is what my wife told me. She said the Cardinal had enticed Buckingham to Paris to ruin the Queen.

CARDINAL. She told you that?

BONACIEUX. Yes, your Eminence. But I scolded her very severely. I said the Cardinal would never dream of such a . . .

CARDINAL. Hold your tongue. You're an imbecile.

BONACIEUX. That's just what she said.

CARDINAL. I need your assistance, my dear Bonacieux. Your wife has left custody. I want you to go back home and wait for her. She may suspect a trap: you can reassure her. Then my men will bring her to see me and I can give her some fatherly advice.

BONACIEUX. Please tell her to keep out of mischief, Your Eminence. She won't listen to me.

CARDINAL. She'll be in good hands. And Bonacieux, I hope you won't hold your night in the Bastille against me.

BONACIEUX. No, no.

CARDINAL. If you ever come by any information—let me know. I pay well for loyal service. Bicarat: escort M. Bonacieux home. (*Bonacieux leaves with Bicarat. Through another entrance, Milady appears.*) Milady, how refreshing to deal with someone of intelligence. But no sooner do I have the pleasure of your company than I have to send you away again.

MILADY. You intend to extract the full pound of flesh, Your Eminence.

CARDNIAL. I keep my word, Milady. The Château de la Fère will be yours.

MILADY. But when will I be free to enjoy it?

CARDINAL. Milady, you agreed to my terms. I'd be sorry to see you go back on them. I've enjoyed working with you.

MILADY. And I would hate to deny you any pleasure.

CARDINAL. So: this is your safe conduct to England: you leave tonight. Get yourself invited to the next ball the Duke of Buckingham attends. He'll be wearing a set of twelve diamonds. Cut off two, and bring them to me immediately. If there's any change of plan, the Comte de Wardes will bring instructions.

MILADY. Your Eminence, the Duke of Buckingham regards me as an enemy. It won't be easy to get close to him.

CARDINAL. The Duke's appetites are fierce. You have made colder men your victims.

SCENE 10

Bonacieux's shop.
D'Artagnan is in his apartment above, having his boots polished by Planchet. Bicarat and the Guards are concealed below. A knock.

CONSTANCE. Is anyone at home?

BONACIEUX. I am, my dear. I've been waiting up for you.

CONSTANCE. Are you alone?

BONACIEUX. What a silly question, my dear, of course I'm quite alone. (*Constance enters.*) I went to meet you last night and M. Laporte told me—abducted.

CONSTANCE. Yes. I managed to escape.

BONACIEUX. What did they want?

CONSTANCE. Mind your own business. Do you think I'd risk you blurting out the Queen's secret?

BICARAT. (*Coming out of hiding.*) Would you rather discuss it with the Cardinal?

CONSTANCE. Who are you? Who are these men? I'm the mistress of the house—I'm Madame Bonacieux, I serve the Queen.

D'ARTAGNAN. (*Above.*) Madame Bonacieux!

BICARAT. You may find you've served the King and the Cardinal badly by serving the Queen so well. Tie her up.

CONSTANCE. No, no—help!

D'ARTAGNAN. Molesting a woman! Scoundrels! Planchet, my sword.

PLANCHET. Where are you going?

D'ARTAGNAN. Through the trapdoor. (*He goes down.*)

PLANCHET. Oh, sir, you'll get yourself killed.

BICARAT. D'Artagnan! Guards!

CONSTANCE. Help, help!

BONACIEUX. (*Under the fight.*) Hey! You can't carry on like this in my shop. This is private property. Get off, I'll tell the Cardinal. I give you fifty crowns, and you do this to me. I don't need your help any more, do you hear? My prize Normandy cheese, skewered like a chestnut. (*D'Artagnan ousts the Guards, Bicarat and Bonacieux. Then he turns to Constance.*)

D'ARTAGNAN. Have those monsters hurt you?

CONSTANCE. No, only frightened me a little. Thank you for saving me—but who are you?

D'ARTAGNAN. D'Artagnan, Madame, a cadet in the King's Musketeers—at your service.

CONSTANCE. But why are you here? And why was my husband with those men?

D'ARTAGNAN. I live in the apartment upstairs. Yesterday, the Cardinal's Guards arrested him. They must have forced him back here to trap you.

CONSTANCE. But what crime can they possibly charge him with?

D'ARTAGNAN. Some men might think it a crime to be your husband.

CONSTANCE. And was the man who abducted me working for the Cardinal? A tall, dark man who never smiled, with a scar on his left temple?

D'ARTAGNAN. He is the Comte de Rochefort, the Cardinal's agent.

CONSTANCE. Then we have been betrayed. If the Cardinal knows about the diamonds, the Queen is in terrible danger. I must get a message to her.

D'ARTAGNAN. Write it now—I'll take it.

CONSTANCE. The streets are patrolled—it's a long way.

D'ARTAGNAN. I'd take it to the ends of the world for you.

CONSTANCE. Knock at the gate in the Rue de la Harpe. The password is Amiens. Ask for Germain. Tell him to give this to the Queen's valet, M. Laporte.

D'ARTAGNAN. In the meantime, you'd better go up to my apartment. You'll be safer. And my friends will be here soon—Planchet!

PLANCHET. *(Who has been observing the scene discreetly.)* Sir?

D'ARTAGNAN. Go and warn Athos.

CONSTANCE. You know you're risking your life?

D'ARTAGNAN. Madame, God has set me to watch over you. I am always at the Queen's service. And always at yours.

SCENE 11

The Louvre.
The King and the Cardinal are playing chess. Jussac is in attendance.

CARDINAL. Still in check, Your Majesty.

KING. So I am. *(He tries a move.)*

CARDINAL. If you move there, my bishop takes your Queen.

KING. But you'll have to sacrifice a knight. How's that arm of Jussac's, by the way? Still in a sling, I see. Quite a swordsman, young D'Artagnan.

CARDINAL. I hope he proves as brave in war as he does in a private brawl.

KING. What are you hinting at? And check yourself.

CARDINAL. That the English may land at La Rochelle. Then we'll have a full-scale campaign on our hands. Check, Your Majesty, and mate. The Duke of Buckingham was in Paris last week.

KING. Buckingham! What's he been up to?

CARDINAL. Your guess is as good as mine. Some sort of intrigue, of course, with the Protestants at La Rochelle, or with the agents of Spain.

KING. You're hiding something from me. She's been deceiving me.

CARDINAL. What a vile accusation, Sire. The Queen is virtue personified. And all France knows how much she loves your Majesty.

KING. Women are notoriously weak, Monseigneur, as your hours in the Confessional must have taught you. And I consider myself a better judge of the Queen's affections than you or France.

34

CARDINAL. I still maintain the Duke was only making political mischief.

KING. And I'm convinced his mission was more personal. But we'll get to the bottom of it; and if the Queen's guilty she'd better take to her knees. She'll need all the help she can muster.

CARDINAL. I find the mere suspicion of such a crime quite repugnant. But if Your Majesty insists, I suppose we must consider it. Dona Estefania did inform me that Her Majesty has been writing letters all evening.

KING. To her lover, of course. We must read them.

CARDINAL. How can we possibly obtain them? It's hardly a suitable task for Your Majesty, or myself, for that matter.

KING. Order a search. First her apartments, then her person.

CARDINAL. We are discussing Anne of Austria, Queen of France . . .

KING. If she's forgotten her position, she'll be treated as she deserves. Have it done.

CARDINAL. Very well, Your Majesty. Jussac, search the Queen's apartments for any documents; and inform the Queen that His Majesty requests her presence. (*Jussac exits.*)

KING. Has she deceived me?

CARDINAL. I believe she's been intriguing against Your Majesty's state, but not your honour.

KING. Against both. She's never loved me. And she's besotted by that Machiavel. Where did they meet this time?

CARDINAL. There was no meeting.

KING. You seem to be singularly well acquainted with the Duke's movements, Monseigneur. May one enquire why you didn't arrest him?

CARDINAL. Arrest the King of England's Chief Minister! That would cause an international scandal. And suppose Your Majesty's suspicions proved true? You'd be the laughing stock of Europe. (*Jussac returns with the Queen, who is accompanied by M. Laporte and Estefania.*)

JUSSAC. Her Majesty, the Queen.

ANNE. A peremptory summons for this hour of the night, Sire. And what does this man's search mean? Do you think my apartment hides anything I would be ashamed to give you?

KING. I won't tell you what I think or don't think until I choose,

Madame. I have reason to believe you wrote a letter tonight. Apparently it's not in your writing desk. I should like to read it.

CARDINAL. Madame, have you written a letter tonight?

ANNE. I have, Monsiegneur. It's here. (*She indicates her bosom.*)

CARDINAL. Jussac. The letter. (*Jussac approaches.*)

ANNE. You heard His Eminence. You must be bolder. (*He makes a grab for it. She forestalls him. He takes the letter to the King.*)

KING. Monseigneur, the Queen doesn't like you. She asks her brother, the King of Spain, to declare war, and make your dismissal a condition of peace. Would Your Majesty be good enough to withdraw for a few moments? I have an important matter of politics to discuss. (*Queen and Estefania withdraw.*) Well, Monseigneur, you were right and I was wrong. Nothing but politics. And all to do with you.

CARDINAL. Your Majesty, perhaps the time has come for me to resign. You see to what lengths my opponents are prepared to go. As I've mentioned many times, my health has suffered: I'm very willing to hand over the burdens of office to someone else.

KING. I understand you perfectly, Monseigneur, and I will not hear of it. But I fully appreciate the difficulties of your position: everyone implicated in this letter will be punished, including the Queen.

CARDINAL. God forbid the Queen should suffer on my account. She looks on me as an enemy, I know, even though I've often defended her against you. If she's been unfaithful to you, that would be different, and I'd be the first to condemn her. But now she's proved herself a loving wife. Your Majesty has been rather harsh with her: it would be a graceful gesture if you healed the breach.

KING. I—ask her pardon?

CARDINAL. Sire, it is blessed to forgive. Do something to give her pleasure. You know how she loves dancing—hold a ball in her honour.

KING. You know how such entertainments bore me.

CARDINAL. Then she'll be all the more grateful to you.

KING. Madame! (*The Queen returns.*) I have something to say to you. It occurs to me that life at Court has been rather tedious these last few months. Mostly the Cardinal's fault, of course, pestering me at all hours of the day and night with affairs of state. So I thought we would have a little celebration. In fact, I've decided to hold a gala ball a week from Saturday. How does that please you, Madame?

ANNE. Very much. I haven't had an opportunity to dance for months.

CARDINAL. Or an opportunity to wear the diamonds Your Majesty was given by the nation.

KING. An excellent suggestion, Monseigneur. You haven't worn them since your birthday. You hear, Madame?

ANNE. Yes, sire.

KING. You'll appear at my ball?

ANNE. Yes, sire.

KING. Wearing the diamonds?

ANNE. Yes, sire.

KING. Thank you, Madame. That's all I have to say to you. Goodnight. (*The King, Cardinal, Jussac leave. The Queen turns to Laporte and Estefania for support. A Guard enters with a message for Laporte.*)

ANNE. I have been betrayed—the Cardinal knows everything.

LAPORTE. Your Majesty—a message from Madame Bonacieux.

ANNE. Who brought it?

LAPORTE. A cadet in the Musketeers. He's still at the gate. Tell him to wait. (*The Guard goes. Dona Estefania is creeping off.*) Dona Estefania! Stay here. Your Majesty, someone must go to the Duke. We still have a chance. (*They go.*)

SCENE 12

Bonacieux' shop.
Bonacieux is in a cupboard: Constance upstairs. D'Artagnan enters.

D'ARTAGNAN. Constance!

CONSTANCE. (*Above.*) Thank God you're safe. (*She comes down.*)

D'ARTAGNAN. I saw M. Laporte. He's given me a letter from

37

the Queen. (*Constance stretches out a hand.*) It has to be delivered to the Duke of Buckingham in London.

CONSTANCE. By whom?

D'ARTAGNAN. By whoever you choose. Constance, if the Queen needs a loyal, brave, intelligent man, I have at least two of these qualifications.

CONSTANCE. And what pledge can you give me?

D'ARTAGNAN. My love for you.

CONSTANCE. So you say.

D'ARTAGNAN. Haven't I given you proof already?

CONSTANCE. I'll trust you, D'Artagnan. You're brave, I know. You say you love me. Time will tell. But I promise you, if you fail me in any way, you'll never see me again alive.

D'ARTAGNAN. And I promise you: if I'm captured, I'll die rather than say one word which might harm you or the Queen.

CONSTANCE. What about your regiment?

D'ARTAGNAN. That's all arranged. I felt sure you'd trust me, so I called to see M. de Tréville on my way back.

CONSTANCE. And money?

D'ARTAGNAN. I haven't thought of that.

CONSTANCE. Here are the keys to my husband's chest. Help yourself. (*Athos enters, reading a note.*)

ATHOS. "My dear Athos, please take a fortnight's leave for the good of your health. Drink the waters at some spa and give your liver a chance. De Tréville." Can you explain this, D'Artagnan? Good evening, Madame. (*Aramis and Porthos rush in, followed by Planchet.*)

ARAMIS. Since when are Musketeers given leave without applying for it?

D'ARTAGNAN. Since they acquired friends who apply for them. Constance—allow me to present—Athos, Porthos, and Aramis—Madame Bonacieux.

ALL. Madame.

ARAMIS. So where are we going?

D'ARTAGNAN. London. (*He hands out money.*)

PORTHOS. What in the world for?

D'ARTAGNAN. You'll have to take my word there's an excellent reason. Besides, we may not all get there.

ARAMIS. So it's a campaign.

PORTHOS. If I'm risking my skin, I prefer to know why.

D'ARTAGNAN. Does the King give you reasons?

ATHOS. D'Artagnan's quite right. We have two weeks' leave and two hundred crowns; so let's go and get ourselves killed.

D'ARTAGNAN. Planchet, saddle the horses.

PORTHOS. But we haven't made a plan. Where are we heading for?

D'ARTAGNAN, Calais.

PORTHOS. Here's my advice. Four men riding together are highly suspicious. I'll travel via Boulogne. Athos will set out an hour later and head for Amiens. Aramis for Noyon. D'Artagnan must take another route and disguise himself as Planchet. Planchet will . . .

ATHOS. Porthos, never trust a servant that far. Secrets may occasionally be betrayed by a gentleman, but they're invariably sold by servants.

D'ARTAGNAN. Porthos' whole plan is impractical. Look: I've been entrusted with a sealed letter for the Duke of Buckingham. If I'm killed, one of you must take it and so on. As long as one of us arrives, the Queen will be saved.

ATHOS. All the same, we'd better leave Paris separately. Let's meet at Chantilly—at the Shoulder of Mutton.

D'ARTAGNAN. But first, we must escort Constance to the Louvre. (*They troop out. Bonacieux emerges from the cupboard.*)

BONACIEUX. The little hussy! And she gave him my money. The Shoulder of Mutton at Chantilly—I must tell my friend, the Cardinal.

SCENE 13

The Shoulder of Mutton at Chantilly.
A stranger comes on with the Innkeeper. He sits slumped at a table.

INNKEEPER. This is the last time you come here—breaking up the place.

STRANGER. Cardinal's orders. You'll be paid.

INNKEEPER. I didn't get paid last time. Every time you come here it's the same thing.

STRANGER. Silence. Release that pigeon and get out of here. They're coming. (*Porthos, D'Artagnan, Aramis, Athos enter.*)
PORTHOS. Breakfast for four, landlord! You always get a good meal at the Shoulder of Mutton. Remember that dinner last summer?
ARAMIS. Delicious.
PORTHOS. Lobster . . .
D'ARTAGNAN. Normandy?
PORTHOS. And then quail. I must have put away a dozen. (*Innkeeper comes through with a pigeon.*) What's that, a pigeon? Roast pigeon and Burgundy. (*Porthos picks up a tankard.*)
STRANGER. To the Cardinal's health!
PORTHOS. If you'll drink to the King's.
STRANGER. I recognize no King but the Cardinal!
PORTHOS. Then you're a drunken ass. (*The stranger draws.*) Aramis, Athos, D'Artagnan—ride on. I'll catch you up. (*D'Artagnan, Athos and Aramis leave. Porthos is finally wounded in the behind.*)
STRANGER. What's your name?
PORTHOS. Porthos.
STRANGER. Not D'Artagnan?
PORTHOS. No, damn it, Porthos. (*The stranger leaves. The Innkeeper helps Porthos off.*)

SCENE 14

A Bridge. Crèvecoeur.
Bicarat and workmen enter and set up a bridge.

D'ARTAGNAN. No sign of Porthos.
ATHOS. Well, that leaves three.
ARAMIS. But why did he pick on Porthos?
D'ARTAGNAN. Porthos talks the most, so he presumed he was the leader.
WORKMAN. The bridge is unsafe. You'll have to go round.
ATHOS. We'll cross here. The servants can take the horses around by the ford.
ARAMIS. Clear a way and let us pass.
WORKMAN. Can't be done. You can swim the river.
ARAMIS. Insolent scum—out of our way. (*Workmen produce*

muskets.) Ride on, Athos, D'Artagnan—I'll hold them off. (*He kills one.*) Requiescat in pace. (*Aramis bars the way until he falls, wounded by a musket ball. The others fight their way across, followed by Planchet and Bicarat.*)

SCENE 15

The Gilded Lily at Amiens.
Athos and D'Artagnan enter, with Planchet and Grimaud.

ATHOS. We must swallow our pride from now on, D'Artagnan; take our hats off to peasants, smile sweetly at landladies. (*The Landlady comes in with a pigeon, hastily concealing the note.*)
PLANCHET. Haven't we seen that pigeon somewhere before?
ATHOS. Nonsense, Planchet, you're getting jumpy. Are the horses fed and watered, Landlady? We'll settle the bill, then, and be off.
LANDLADY. That's two francs for the horses, two francs for the wine, five francs for the dinner, three francs for the tax. That's sixteen francs, sir. (*He hands over money.*)
ATHOS. Keep the change.
LANDLADY. These are forgeries. Arrest them!
ATHOS. I'll slice your ears off. (*Guards burst in. A fight.*) Ride on, D'Artagnan. (*D'Artagnan goes with Planchet. Athos produces two pistols. A gunfight. Finally, he and Grimaud go down to the cellar, shutting the trapdoor after them. The Landlady stands over it in despair.*)
LANDLADY. Come up, sir. Please come up. All my supplies are down there!

SCENE 16

Windsor Castle.
Music is playing. The Duke of Buckingham waltzes in with Milady. He is wearing the diamonds.

MILADY. Why have we left the ballroom?
BUCKINGHAM. I prefer moonlight to candlelight, though I didn't

41

anticipate a walk in Windsor Park with you, Milady. I thought we were enemies.

MILADY. Sometimes we try to avoid what we're really drawn to.

BUCKINGHAM. You make up a quarrel so beautifully, my dear. We must quarrel again soon.

MILADY. Shall I start?

BUCKINGHAM. Not yet, my dear. We haven't finished the reconciliation. Come. (*As he leads her off, she flourishes a pair of scissors.*)

SCENE 17

Calais—the harbour.
The Comte de Wardes accosts a Sea-Captain. D'Artagnan and Planchet arive in time to overhear.

DE WARDES. My man—Captain—I'm looking for a passage to England.

SEA CAPTAIN. Are you now? Well, I'm sailing there in an hour.

DE WARDES. That suits me admirably.

SEA CAPTAIN. It may do. But I'll be sailing without you. The order was posted this morning—no passengers without a signed permit from the Cardinal.

DE WARDES. I have one . . . I'll come aboard at once.

SEA CAPTAIN. You'll need the harbourmaster's endorsement—that's his office on the next quay. (*The Captain leaves. D'Artagnan confronts de Wardes.*)

D'ARTAGNAN. You're in a hurry, Monsieur.

DE WARDES. Yes, I am.

D'ARTAGNAN. I'm sorry to hear that. I'm in a great hurry too, and I wanted to ask you a favour.

DE WARDES. Well, what is it?

D'ARTAGNAN. I need your permit. It seems to be essential, and I haven't got one.

DE WARDES. Do you know who I am? I'm the Comte de Wardes, in the Cardinal's service. Out of my way, and let me pass.

D'ARTAGNAN. And I am D'Artagnan, in my own service (*He draws.*)

DE WARDES. Then I shall have to kill you. (*They fight.*

42

D'Artagnan wins and stabs de Wardes three times, crying with each thrust:)
D'ARTAGNAN. One for Porthos; one for Aramis; and one for Athos. *(The Comte collapses. D'Artagnan is bending over to remove the permit when the Comte revives momentarily.)*
DE WARDES. And one for you.
D'ARTAGNAN. And one from me.
DE WARDES. Help! Murder! *(He staggers off.)*
PLANCHET. O, sir, you're wounded.
D'ARTAGNAN. It's nothing. Now—first to the harbourmaster; and then—to England. *(Milady passes.)* I wonder what Milady's doing in Calais?

SCENE 18

D'Artagnan enters with Buckingham and the servant, Patrick.

D'ARTAGNAN. My lord! A letter from the Queen of France.
BUCKINGHAM. The first letter she's ever sent me. I'm grateful, Monsieur. *(D'Artagnan hands the letter over.)*
PATRICK. Monsieur, there's blood on your jacket.
D'ARTAGNAN. It's only a scratch.
BUCKINGHAM. Then she must have the diamonds back. Patrick— *(Patrick goes to a veiled altar.)* If you ever get the chance, tell Her Majesty what you're about to see. *(The curtain is drawn, revealing a full-length portrait of the Queen, below it an altar, and on a cushion, the diamonds. The Duke kneels for a moment, then takes the diamonds.)* These are the most precious things the Queen possessed: so you can imagine how infinitely more precious they are to me. But if she needs them, you must take them to her. Her will be done. *(He kisses them, then cries out.)* No!
D'ARTAGNAN. My lord?
BUCKINGHAM. Two are missing.
D'ARTAGNAN. Lost—or stolen?
BUCKINGHAM. Stolen—look!

43

PATRICK. My lord, you've only worn them once, at Windsor two nights ago.

BUCKINGHAM. It can only have been the Comtesse de Winter—and she must therefore be an agent of Richelieu's. When does this ball take place?

D'ARTAGNAN. Saturday.

BUCKINGHAM. Five days. There's still time. Patrick, send for my jeweller. Tell him to bring his paraphernalia. And write out an order: no ship is to sail for France from any British port. (*Patrick goes.*) It will be interpreted as the first step towards a declaration of war. But when those diamonds return to France, my hands are free to do what my heart suggests. (*Patrick returns with Mr. O'Reilly, the jeweller.*) Mr. O'Reilly, how much is one of these diamonds worth?

O'REILLY. Three thousand pounds, your Grace.

BUCKINGHAM. And how long would it take you to make two replicas?

O'REILLY. Five days, your Grace.

BUCKINGHAM. I'll give you three thousand pounds a piece if you can do it in two.

O'REILLY. Then you'll have them, your Grace.

BUCKINGHAM. You're a practical man, Mr. O'Reilly. There are one or two conditions: the diamonds cannot leave this room.

O'REILLY. Can't be done, your Grace. I'm the only man in the country who could do it for you—the only man in the whole world for that matter.

BUCKINGHAM. Precisely. So you can't leave the room either. We'll send for anything you need, assistants, stones . . .

O'REILLY. What about me wife?

BUCKINGHAM. She can come too. Patrick, see to it at once.

PATRICK. This way, sir. (*Patrick leads O'Reilly aside.*)

BUCKINGHAM. Now, my friend, I hope you'll stay and dine with me. We should discuss arrangements for your journey back. And you must tell me how I can repay you—I'm in your debt.

D'ARTAGNAN. My Lord, I am doing this, not for your sake, but for the Queen's; and for someone else who . . .

BUCKINGHAM. I think I can guess. You're a lucky man, D'Artagnan. Little Madame . . .

D'ARTAGNAN. My Lord, I haven't named her. As I said, to

me, you're just an Englishman, and an enemy. I should infinitely prefer to meet you on the field of battle than in a palace apartment.
BUCKINGHAM. We have a saying: "Proud as a Scotsman."
D'ARTAGNAN. We say "Proud as a Gascon." The Gascons are the Scots of France. (*They leave. O'Reilly grinds away.*)

SCENE 19

The Louvre.
A room near the ballroom—music. Lords and Ladies in evening dress. The Cardinal, attended by Jussac, is pacing up and down. Then Rochefort escorts in Milady. She hands him a package. He opens it, smiles: she curtseys to him and moves back. Tan-tan-tara. "His Majesty the King." Tan-tan-tara, "Her Majesty the Queen." The King and Queen, attended, enter from different doors. Everyone bows and curtseys. The Queen is not wearing her diamonds. The Cardinal goes over to the King and whispers.

LOUIS. Why, Madame, have you neglected to wear your diamonds?
ANNE. I was afraid I might lose them in the dancing.
LOUIS. Those diamonds were given to you by the people: they are to be worn in the people's presence. Your jewellery is intended to compliment your beauty, not to be hoarded in boxes.
ANNE. Sire, I will send for them. My only wish is to please Your Majesty.
LOUIS. Then do so, Madame, and at once. (*The Queen and her women withdraw.*)
CARDINAL. Your Majesty, I have something that will interest you. (*He gives him the two diamonds.*)
LOUIS. What in the world are these?
CARDINAL. If the Queen returns with her diamonds, which I am inclined to doubt, count them. And if you find there are only ten, ask her who could have stolen these two. (*The Queen returns. And music strikes up for a dance. During it, the King tries to count the diamonds, without success. The Queen covers them with her hand. The dance ends.*)

45

LOUIS. Madame. I must thank you for complying with my wishes. But I suspect two of the diamonds are missing. I should like to restore them.

ANNE. What do you mean, Sire? Now I shall have fourteen. *(She takes her hand away.)*

LOUIS. *(In the background, D'Artagnan appears.)* Monseigneur, explain yourself.

CARDINAL. Your Majesty, I wanted to give the Queen these diamonds as tokens of my respect and admiration. But I felt it was presumptuous to offer them to her myself. By this means I hoped to persuade her acceptance.

ANNE. I'm delighted to accept them, Monseigneur. But you shouldn't be so extravagant. I'm sure these two have cost you more than the original twelve. And now, Sire, shall we make our appearance in the Grand ballroom? Lead the way, Monseigneur. *(Everyone processes out, except Constance. D'Artagnan comes forward, attended by Laporte. He moves towards Constance, Laporte restrains him. The Queen re-enters momentarily.)*

LAPORTE. M. D'Artagnan—the Queen. *(The Queen gives D'Artagnan her hand to kiss and a ring. She leaves. Again D'Artagnan moves towards Constance, again Laporte restrains him and leads him out. Jussac and Bicarat enter. The Cardinal appears and signals to them. They seize Constance and carry her off. A piercing scream.)*

ACT TWO

SCENE 20

Various locations: the beginning of a campaign.
Buckingham and Patrick enter.

BUCKINGHAM. Order my secretary to write a memorandum to the King, Patrick. The conscience of the English people can no longer ignore the sufferings of our Protestant brethren in La Rochelle. And issue instructions to the Admiralty: Assemble our squadrons at Portsmouth. We declare war on France. *(They leave. Rochefort and the Cardinal enter.)*

ROCHEFORT. Buckingham has declared war, your Eminence. The English fleet lies at Portsmouth, under orders to sail for La Rochelle.

CARDINAL. I intend to supervise the siege operations in person, Rochefort—as soon as I can persuade His Majesty to leave Paris. Since the ball, he has renewed his pleasure in the Queen's company. In that connection, have you secured Madame Bonacieux?

ROCHEFORT. She is in Mantes jail, your Eminence.

CARDINAL. Make certain she stays there. As for hèr admirer, have Jussac call at his lodging. It's time that young Gascon came to work for me. (*They leave. De Tréville enters with D'Artagnan.*)

DE TRÉVILLE. Now, D'Artagnan, your triumphant return is obviously connected with the Queen's delight and the Cardinal's humiliation.

D'ARTAGNAN. Can the Cardinal know that I've been in London?

DE TRÉVILLE. The devil—in London! And is that where you came by that diamond shining like a lighthouse on your finger?

D'ARTAGNAN. Sir, this diamond was given to me by the Queen.

DE TRÉVILLE. Sell it. Money is anonymous. That ring's pedigree could hang you.

D'ARTAGNAN. Sell a ring given to me by my Queen? Never.

DE TRÉVILLE. Then have the sense to turn the stone inwards. A Gascon doesn't light on such treasures in his mother's jewel-box. The Cardinal has a long memory, and a longer arm, as you doubtless discovered. Which reminds me—where are your three companions?

D'ARTAGNAN. I left them on the road.

DE TRÉVILLE. Then go and find them while the Cardinal hunts for you in Paris. We march for La Rochelle within the week.

D'ARTAGNAN. But sir—I must look for my mistress.

DE TRÉVILLE. My young friend, it was by woman that man first fell. Believe me. Go tonight. (*D'Artagnan bows assent, as de Tréville leaves. Jussac passes by. Planchet appears.*)

D'ARTAGNAN. M. Jussac?

PLANCHET. The very man. Oh, he was all milk and honey, Monsieur. "I have come on his Eminence's behalf, who sends his compliments, and would be vastly obliged if M. D'Artagnan will pay him a visit at the Palais-Royal."

D'ARTAGNAN. And how did you reply?

PLANCHET. That you were out—as he could see for himself. "Where has he gone?" asked M. Jussac. "To Gascony," I replied, "to visit his aged father before he leaves for the wars." You see, Monsieur, not being a gentleman, I thought I might be permitted to lie.

D'ARTAGNAN. Planchet, you almost told the truth. We leave in ten minutes. Saddle the horses.

PLANCHET. So we're to be chopped and peppered all. over again?

D'ARTAGNAN. Take your musket and pistols.

PLANCHET. There! What did I say?

D'ARTAGNAN. Calm yourself. This is a pleasure excursion.

PLANCHET. Just like the one last week, when it rained musket-balls and man-traps.

D'ARTAGNAN. Are you afraid, Planchet? (*He goes.*)

PLANCHET. Afraid, Monsieur? A Planchet from Picardy?

SCENE 21

The Shoulder of Mutton: Chantilly.
Porthos is recuperating from his wound in a wheel-chair.
D'Artagnan joins him.

D'ARTAGNAN. Porthos!

PORTHOS. D'Artagnan, you're alive! Forgive my not getting up— I don't suppose you've heard about my unfortunate accident?

D'ARTAGNAN. Not a word.

PORTHOS. I was making mincemeat of my opponents—two of them took to their heels, I was just about to deliver the coup de grace to a third when I slipped and fell. I twisted my ankle very severely.

D'ARTAGNAN. And what became of your opponent?

PORTHOS. He made an extremely fortunate escape

D'ARTAGNAN. So you're out of action just when we're at war with England.

PORTHOS. At war?

D'ARTAGNAN. M. de Tréville has ordered you to report back for duty—we're being posted to La Rochelle.

PORTHOS. A campaign? Then I must get back to Paris— I need a

new outfit. But I'm in a slightly embarrassing position here, D'Artagnan. I lost all my money gambling and I can't pay my bill.
D'ARTAGNAN. Surely your Duchess will send you something?
PORTHOS. You won't believe what vile luck I'm having, my dear D'Artagnan. I wrote to her and had no reply! She must be at her estate in the country. (*He hands D'Artagnan a bill.*)
D'ARTAGNAN. I can settle this temporarily, and you can pay me back when you next see your Duchess. What's this item—medical expenses?
PORTHOS. A course of massage—for my knee.
D'ARTAGNAN. We'll meet in Paris, then. I'll ride on to Crèvecoeur and find Aramis. (*He leaves.*)
PORTHOS. But surely you'll stay for dinner? They do a first-class rabbit stew. . . .

SCENE 22

The Black Lion: Crèvecoeur.
Planchet joins D'Artagnan outside the room where Aramis, in black gown and cap, is in conference with two priests. He is surrounded by theological books.

PLANCHET. M. Aramis is not to be disturbed.
D'ARTAGNAN. Then he has a lady with him.
PLANCHET. Monsieur! A priest—two priests.
D'ARTAGNAN. Good heavens! He must be dying. (*D'Artagnan bursts into the room.*)
ARAMIS. My dear friend, I am delighted to see you safe and well.
D'ARTAGNAN. I'm equally delighted to see you, Aramis. If it is Aramis.
ARAMIS. Who else?
D'ARTAGNAN. At first I feared you were on your deathbed. Now I presume I have stumbled upon a seminary. Don't let me intrude if you're making your confession.
ARAMIS. No intrusion in the least. My friend has lately been delivered from most perilous circumstances.
DIVINES. Praise be to God, Monsieur.
D'ARTAGNAN. I have already done so, your Reverences.

49

ARAMIS. Come and assist in our discussion. These gentlemen are giving me guidance about my thesis.

D'ARTAGNAN. Thesis? What thesis?

ARAMIS. Surely even you must know that a thesis has to be submitted before the ordination examination. They consider it should be on dogma, and suggest as a subject: "Utraque manus in benedicendo clericis inferioribus necessaria est."

JESUIT. The lesser orders of priests must use both hands when they give the blessing. An admirable subject.

CURÉ. Admirable, and thoroughly dogmatical.

JESUIT. Let us consider what the Gospel says: Imponite manus—place the hands, not manum, the hand: place the hands.

CURÉ. Place the hands.

JESUIT. But St. Peter, from whom the Popes derive their authority, writes—porrige digitos—the fingers.

CURÉ. Digitos—the fingers.

D'ARTAGNAN. The Devil take you and your Latin.

JESUIT. My friend, we will retire temporarily. Let us hope our seed has not fallen on stony ground, or aves coeli commederunt illam, the birds of the air will devour it. We shall sing a special Mass for you. (*The Divines leave.*)

ARAMIS. You perceive I have returned to my former calling. My wound was a warning from heaven— Grace brushed my soul and summoned me to renounce the lusts of the flesh.

D'ARTAGNAN. Then Grace has most unfortunate timing. France is at war with England. The Musketeers are to march on La Rochelle! At least let's have dinner and talk things over.

ARAMIS. You won't mind sharing my frugal meal? You must remember it's Friday, so I have only ordered a simple dish of spinach.

D'ARTAGNAN. Spinach!

ARAMIS. Mortify the flesh, D'Artagnan. And if your body does not benefit, your soul certainly will.

D'ARTAGNAN. Aramis, for the last time, are you serious?

ARAMIS. On sacred matters, I do not jest.

D'ARTAGNAN. Betray your regiment, renounce your friends?

ARAMIS. Tomorrow, you and Porthos and Aramis will be faint shadows.

D'ARTAGNAN. And your mistress?

ARAMIS. Vanitas vanitatum. Où sont les neiges d'Antan?

D'ARTAGNAN. In that case, I shall have to burn this letter.
ARAMIS. What letter?
D'ARTAGNAN. Oh, a letter which was sent to your lodgings, from some broken-hearted girl—Madame de Chevreuse's chambermaid, perhaps, who stole a sheet of scented paper and sealed her missive with a Duchess' coronet . . .
ARAMIS. Give it to me.
D'ARTAGNAN. I must have lost it. But, as you say, men, and no doubt women too, are only shadows, and love mere vanity.
ARAMIS. D'Artagnan, you're torturing me.
D'ARTAGNAN. Oh, here it is. (*Aramis tears it from him and reads it.*) The chambermaid has a sense of style?
ARAMIS. She loves me. She still loves me. She had to return to Tours. She keeps faith with me.
PLANCHET. (*Entering with the spinach.*) Your dinner, Monsieur.
ARAMIS. Take that revolting pap away. We'll have a larded hare, a stuffed capon, a leg of mutton with garlic, and four bottles of Burgundy. Oh, D'Artagnan, you have resurrected me!

SCENE 23

The Gilded Lily: Amiens.
The Landlady is crouched by the cellar door. Below, a pandemonium of raucous singing, banging, and the splintering of glass. Lord de Winter and Lord Ormsby wait impatiently.

LANDLADY. Come up, Monsieur—for the love of God, Monsieur . . .
DE WINTER. This is monstrous.
ORMSBY. Insupportable. (*D'Artagnan and Planchet arrive.*)
DE WINTER. The man must be mad. We'll just have to break the door down and kill him if necessary.
D'ARTAGNAN. Messieurs. (*He and Planchet draw their pistols.*) You will kill nobody, if you please. Planchet, keep your eye on them.
ATHOS. (*From below.*) D'Artagnan, is that really you?
D'ARTAGNAN. Yes, my friend.
ATHOS. Bravo. Then we can teach these English door-breakers a

51

lesson. (*Ormsby gives a defiant kick at the door.*) Stand back, D'Artagnan—I'm going to shoot.

D'ARTAGNAN. Gentlemen, sheathe your swords and be patient for a moment. My friend and I will be honoured to meet you in due course. Athos, open the door, I beg of you. (*Crashing and heaving. The door opens. Athos, dishevelled and dissipated, staggers out.*) You're wounded.

ATHOS. Not a scratch. Just dead drunk. Landlady, I congratulate you on your admirable cellar. I must have tasted my way through a hundred bottles.

LANDLADY. Good God! The man's a sponge. If the servant's drunk half as much, I'm ruined. (*Grimaud emerges, tottering, soused in wine and oil.*)

ATHOS. Grimaud would not dream of faring so well as his master. He only drank from the barrel. Listen. He can't have turned the tap off.

LANDLADY. (*Investigating.*) The cellar's awash . . .

ATHOS. And now, my English friends, you were rash enough to talk in terms of killing us.

DE WINTER. Then let us introduce ourselves. Lord de Winter. Of Sheffield.

D'ARTAGNAN. D'Artagnan. From Gascony.

ORMSBY. The Earl of Ormsby.

ATHOS. Athos.

ORMSBY. But that's not a man's name—it's a mountain.

ATHOS. Then your lordship may deduce it is assumed.

ORMSBY. Monsieur, one only fights with one's equal. (*Athos whispers his name to Ormsby.*)

ATHOS. Am I sufficiently well-bred to cross swords with you? (*Ormsby bows his assent.*) Then let me favour you with another item of information. I am believed to be dead. I have excellent reasons for preserving that belief. So you will understand that I am compelled to kill you. (*They fight. Athos kills Ormsby. D'Artagnan wounds and disarms de Winter, and stands over him with arm upraised.*)

DE WINTER. Now my estates will pass to Milady . . .

D'ARTAGNAN. Milady?

DE WINTER. Milady de Winter, my sister.

D'ARTAGNAN. Then I shall spare your life for her sake.

DE WINTER. I am much obliged to you, Monsieur. You are well acquainted with my sister?

D'ARTAGNAN. I have only had the opportunity of admiring her.

DE WINTER. Are you returning to Paris, Monsieur?

D'ARTAGNAN. Tomorrow.

DE WINTER. I shall be staying at my sister's. (*He hands D'Artagnan a card.*) If you care to call one evening at eight, it will be my pleasure to make the introduction. (*He bows and limps off. Planchet and Grimaud remove the corpse.*)

ATHOS. And now, D'Artagnan, what of the others? (*The Landlady emerges from the cellar.*) More wine, Madame—that Burgundy in the far corner.

LANDLADY. You must have drunk a hundred crowns' worth—you've gnawed my sausages, ravaged my hams—

ATHOS. The quantity of rats down there is disgraceful.

D'ARTAGNAN. Madame, if you persist in these complaints, we shall all four withdraw below to investigate the damage. (*The Landlady capitulates, and descends again with Planchet.*) Athos—I am relieved to find you well. I discovered Porthos laid up with a "twisted knee"—and Aramis disputing with the Jesuits. (*Landlady and Planchet bring wine and ham, and leave.*) They are riding back to Paris directly. Their affairs—prosper.

ATHOS. And what of yours, my friend?

D'ARTAGNAN. The Queen's diamonds were restored to her in time. In other respects, I am less fortunate.

ATHOS. In what way?

D'ARTAGNAN. I'll tell you later.

ATHOS. Why later? Because you imagine I am drunk? My mind is never clearer. Tell me now.

D'ARTAGNAN. Because I have heard nothing of my beloved Constance.

ATHOS. Oh, don't break your heart over a woman.

D'ARTAGNAN. That is easy enough to say, Athos. But you have never been in love.

ATHOS. That is true. I have never been in love.

D'ARTAGNAN. So you should have more sympathy for those who are.

ATHOS. You have all my sympathy: but you're lucky she's vanished while you still believe she loves you. Let me tell you a real love-story. It may open your eyes about women.

D'ARTAGNAN. Is it about you?

ATHOS. About a friend of mine, the Comte de la Fère. His estate's not far from here. When he was twenty-five he fell in love with a girl of sixteen, the most beautiful girl imaginable. She'd recently come to live in the country with her brother, a priest: no one knew where they'd come from, but she was so lovely and her brother so devout, that nobody bothered to find out. My friend the Comte could have seduced her: he exercised le droit de seigneur on his estate. But she captivated him, and fool that he was, he married her.

D'ARTAGNAN. But he loved her!

ATHOS. He loved her then. He took her to his castle, and made her the first lady in the province. And he was as happy as only a man in love with his wife can be. One day, she rode out hunting with him and had a bad fall. She fainted. The Comte loosened her dress, and uncovered her shoulder. And what do you think he saw?

D'ARTAGNAN. How can I tell?

ATHOS. A fleur-de-lis, branded on her flesh by the common hangman. His angel was a devil, a thief who had robbed a church.

D'ARTAGNAN. And what did the Comte do?

ATHOS. He stripped the dress he had given her from her tainted body. He tied her hands behind her, and hanged her from the nearest tree.

D'ARTAGNAN. A murder!

ATHOS. From one point of view. Let's have another drink. Anyway, D'Artagnan, that cured me of beautiful women with long fair hair. It cured my friend too. There's a moral in it somewhere. Love with your head, but never with your heart. More wine, D'Artagnan? (*D'Artagnan's head is buried in his hands: He seems asleep.*) He's a good fellow, but he can't hold his liquor. (*Athos hauls D'Artagnan to his feet, and staggers off.*)

SCENE 24

Milady's Chamber.
Milady and Lord de Winter are at home. A bell rings.
Kitty enters.

KITTY. Milady, a M. D'Artagnan at the gate.

DE WINTER. Ask him to come in. Sister, this is the young

gentleman I told you about— (D'Artagnan is ushered in by Kitty, who gives him an admiring glance.) M. D'Artagnan, who held my life in his hands, and spared me for your sake.

MILADY. Welcome, Monsieur. You have earned the right to my eternal gratitude.

DE WINTER. A remarkable encounter. Ormsby was killed by his opponent's first thrust—and I fared little better!

MILADY. I'm surprised you're so eager to dwell on your humiliation. You will only embarrass M. D'Artagnan. (Kitty enters.)

KITTY. My lord, this has just arrived. (She hands de Winter a note and gazes once more at D'Artagnan.)

DE WINTER. The expected summons, my dear. The Duke of Buckingham seems to require my presence at Portsmouth. M. D'Artagnan—I look forward to renewing our acquaintance. Sister—au revoir. (He kisses Milady and leaves, Kitty also goes.)

MILADY. A glass of wine, Monsieur?

D'ARTAGNAN. Thank you. I've seen you before, Milady.

MILADY. Oh, where?

D'ARTAGNAN. Near Poitiers. You were with the Comte de Rochefort.

MILADY. So you were the young Gascon who challenged him? How splendid.

D'ARTAGNAN. And I saw you two weeks ago at Calais.

MILADY. What a coincidence. On your way to England?

D'ARTAGNAN. Yes, I was.

MILADY. Whatever for?

D'ARTAGNAN. M. de Tréville sent me to buy some horses.

MILADY. Indeed. I find it surprising that such an ambitious, energetic young man isn't in the Cardinal's service.

D'ARTAGNAN. That would be a great honour. But my father knew M. de Tréville, so naturally I applied for the Musketeers.

MILADY. You must be a great asset to them. My brother-in-law may not be very intelligent, but he is an expert swordsman.

D'ARTAGNAN. I thought you were his sister.

MILADY. No: I married his elder brother, who died soon after.

D'ARTAGNAN. I'm sorry. (Milady yawns.) I should go now, but may I come to see you again?

MILADY. By all means. If you don't, I shall have to take steps to arrange it. Kitty!

D'ARTAGNAN. I can find my own way out. Goodnight, Milady.

MILADY. Au revoir, Monsieur.

D'ARTAGNAN. Au revoir. (*Kitty catches him by the arm and leads him upstairs.*)

KITTY. Sh! I must talk to you. Can you spare me a few minutes?

D'ARTAGNAN. Of course, my dear.

KITTY. We won't be overheard up here. It's above Milady's bedroom, but she never goes to sleep before midnight. Are you in love with her?

D'ARTAGNAN. More than I can say.

KITTY. That's very sad.

D'ARTAGNAN. What do you mean?

KITTY. Because she's in love with someone else.

D'ARTAGNAN. How do you know? (*Kitty produces a note.*) To the Comte de Wardes! "I will wait one more night. I am your friend till then. Beware of making me an enemy." Why haven't you delivered this?

KITTY. His servants won't receive it. But you see, Monsieur, there's no hope for you. You have my sympathy, because I know what it is to be in love.

D'ARTAGNAN. Then will you help me?

KITTY. In anything except winning—her love.

D'ARTAGNAN. Why not in that?

KITTY. Because in love it's every girl for herself. (*D'Artagnan realizes what she means. A long kiss.*)

MILADY. Kitty! Kitty! (*Kitty goes downstairs. D'Artagnan remains to overhear.*)

KITTY. Yes, Milady. (*She helps Milady undress.*) I thought that man would never leave.

MILADY. Yes. But he'll be back. I've several scores to settle with that Gascon. To think—he could have killed my brother-in-law, and finally let me inherit the de Winter estates—and he spared his life. What's more, he's already lost me a lot of credit with the Cardinal.

KITTY. You're not in love with him then?

MILADY. Don't be absurd. That bourgeois? Besides, he nearly killed my Comte de Wardes. But I'll have my revenge. That little grocer's wife he was infatuated with has been put away, and I'll deal with him in my own good time .

KITTY. The Comte de Wardes—there's a man, Milady.

MILADY. When I want your opinion, I'll ask for it. Now get to bed.

KITTY. Yes, Milady.

MILADY. And remember, I expect an answer from de Wardes tomorrow. I shall hold you responsible.

KITTY. Of course, Milady. (*She returns to her room.*)

D'ARTAGNAN. That demon!

KITTY. Quiet. She'll hear you. You must go now.

D'ARTAGNAN. I'll be quiet. But first, I'm going to write a reply to that note in the Comte de Warde's name. (*He writes.*) Give her this tomorrow. I'll come at midnight, and you must see that the house is in utter darkness.

KITTY. You can't want to do that after what you've heard.

D'ARTAGNAN. You don't understand. I want to all the more.

KITTY. But you don't love her?

D'ARTAGNAN. No, Kitty, it's you I love. (*He reaches for her. Kitty protests. But realizes that any sound will wake Milady. So she complies.*)

SCENE 25

A Paris church: outside the Confessional.
Organ music. Mme. Coquenard, stalked by Porthos, waits to make her confession.

MME. COQUENARD. (*Clearing her throat.*) M. Porthos.

PORTHOS. (*Feigning surprise.*) Mme. Coquenard! I must be blind not to have seen you. (*He offers her his arm.*)

MME. COQUENARD. I was seated in the next pew, M. Porthos. But you had eyes for no-one but that exquisite beauty—the one you sprinkled with holy water.

PORTHOS. Ah, the Marchese—we are forced to make such rendezvous because of her husband's jealousy.

MME. COQUENARD. M. Porthos, you're a great favourite with the ladies.

PORTHOS. Of course, with a physique like mine, I have my share of fortune.

MME. COQUENARD. Oh, God, how quickly a man forgets.

PORTHOS. Not so quickly as a woman, I fancy, Madame. Weak and helpless, despaired of by surgeons, I lay expiring of wounds and hunger in a mean tavern at Chantilly, with not one answer to my anguished letters—

MME. COQUENARD. M. Porthos . . .

PORTHOS. I who for your sake had abandoned the Comtesse de. . . .

MME. COQUENARD. I know it . . .

PORTHOS. The Baroness de—

MME. COQUENARD. Don't torment me—

PORTHOS. The Duchesse de . . .

MME. COQUENARD. Forgive me, M. Porthos, forgive me. (She kneels before him.) It was my husband who forbade me to send the money. But I have learned my lesson. I promise you, on the next occasion, you will only need to ask. And I dare say you will find the strong-box of an attorney's wife as well-filled as the silk purses of your precious minxes.

PORTHOS. Oh, Madame, if you are rich, that doubles the injury.

MME. COQUENARD. When I say well-filled, you mustn't take me literally.

PORTHOS. Madame, I see you are not truly repentant. I am going to the wars, and something tells me I shall not return . . .

MME. COQUENARD. Be merciful—don't say such things.

PORTHOS. Adieu, Madame. From now until our departure I shall be fully occupied in collecting my equipment. I thought I had friends in Paris, but I see I am sadly mistaken.

MME. COQUENARD. Oh, you have one, M. Porthos—you have one. Come to our house tomorrow. You are my aunt's son—from Picardy—and so my cousin. Come at dinner-time—and be discreet. My husband has his wits about him, for all his seventy years.

PORTHOS. Seventy—that's a great age.

MME. COQUENARD. As you say, M. Porthos. I could be a widow any day. Fortunately, everything's left to me.

PORTHOS. You're a woman to be reckoned with, Mme. Coquenard.

MME. COQUENARD. A demain, my angel.

PORTHOS. À demain, flame of my heart.

Milady's chamber—by candlelight.
Milady, and Kitty, wait to receive their visitor. Midnight
strikes.

MILADY. Read me the Comte's letter again, Kitty. It will help pass the time until he comes.

KITTY. Madame: I did not dare to believe that your first two letters were meant for me. Besides, my wounds kept me in bed. But your third letter, and your servant, convinced me of your love. Tonight at twelve I will come to ask your forgiveness. From the happiest of men, the Comte de Wardes." (*A bell rings.*)

MILADY. Kitty, he's here. Put out the candles, and go to your room. (*D'Artagnan appears.*)

KITTY. The Comte de Wardes. (*She goes.*)

MILADY. Come closer, Comte. You know you are welcome.

D'ARTAGNAN. No-one can see us?

MILADY. I can hardly see your shadow, Comte.

D'ARTAGNAN. I can hardly believe I'm here, Milady. I've dreamed about this from the first moment I saw you—for in that moment I fell in love.

MILADY. And I felt sure that one day we would meet again. Tomorrow, you must give me some pledge of your devotion—and as a token to remind you of me—take this. (*She gives him a ring, and embraces him. D'Artagnan starts.*) My poor angel, savaged by that vicious D'Artagnan—are your wounds still painful?

D'ARTAGNAN. Sometimes—a little.

MILADY. Never fear. I shall have my revenge on him.

D'ARTAGNAN. Don't think about him. Nothing matters now that I have found you at last. Ah, Milady, your hair is like silk—your long, fair hair. (*He leads her towards the bed.*)

SCENE 27

Various locations: letters.
A beggar brings Aramis a letter.

BEGGAR. I wish to speak to a M. Aramis. Is that your name, Monsieur?

ARAMIS. It is. You have brought me a letter? From Tours?

BEGGAR. First, show me a certain handkerchief.

ARAMIS. (*Producing the handkerchief.*) It is here, next to my heart. (*The Beggar hands over the letter, which Aramis opens. The Beggar then produces gold coins from inside his rags, and gives them to Aramis. Aramis reads the letter.*) My friend, Fate decrees that still our paths may not converge. Do your duty at the war; and I will continue to play my part. Accept what the bearer of this letter gives you. Ride into battle equipped like a great Chevalier, and think of me, whose kisses brush your lids in sleep. Adieu, or rather, au revoir. (*The Beggar slips away.*) Welcome my messenger, who is a Grandee of Spain . . . (*Aramis goes. Athos and D'Artagnan meet.*)

ATHOS. D'Artagnan, this Milady of yours seems an infamous creature. But you are wrong to have deceived her. She may prove a terrible enemy. (*He stares at the ring on D'Artagnan's finger.*)

D'ARTAGNAN. You admire my ring?

ATHOS. It's magnificent. It reminds me of a family jewel of my own. Have you sold the Queen's diamond, then?

D'ARTAGNAN. No—this is a gift from my beautiful English mistress. (*A knock. Planchet admits Kitty.*)

KITTY. Monsieur, you must help me. Milady has sent me to the Comte de Wardes, to find out when he means to come again. I must bring her an answer.

ATHOS. D'Artagnan. Renounce this woman.

D'ARTAGNAN. You're right, Athos. I will. (*He writes a note.*) "Do not rely on me, Madame. Since my recovery, I have had a great many affairs of this kind to deal with. When your turn comes round again, I will let you know." (*He seals it, hands it to Kitty, who goes.*) It is beautiful, isn't it? (*He shows Athos his ring.*)

ATHOS. I would not have believed two stones could be so similar. Turn it inwards, D'Artagnan. It brings back painful memories for me.

D'ARTAGNAN. Then I shall sell it, to purchase our equipments. A family jewel, you said . . .

ATHOS. I must be mistaken.

D'ARTAGNAN. And you sold it?

ATHOS. No. I gave it away in a night of love, as you were given yours. (*They go. Kitty returns to Milady.*)

KITTY. Milady—from the Comte de Wardes. (*She hands over the note.*)

MILADY. (*Tearing it open.*) . . . when your turn comes round again! Impossible! That a gentleman should write such a letter! (*Kitty hastens to comfort her.*) Why are you pawing me?

KITTY. I feared Madame was about to faint.

MILADY. I? Faint? What do you take me for? When I am insulted, I avenge myself. Fetch D'Artagnan. Tell him to bring his sword.

SCENE 28

The Coquenards' house: the Procurator's Dinner.
Mme. Coquenard, Coquenard and Porthos are ending a revolting and parsimonious meal served by a starved Apprentice.

COQUENARD. So we're cousins, M. Porthos, or so my wife tells me.

PORTHOS. It appears so, M. Coquenard.

COQUENARD. But only on the female side. (*He waters the wine.*) You spare no expense for your cousin, my dear. An epicurean feast.

PORTHOS. (*Gnawing vainly at his fowl.*) The devil— I respect old age, but not on my plate. (*He chucks the bone over his shoulder.*)

MME. COQUENARD. Can I tempt you, Cousin Porthos, with some of these beans?

PORTHOS. No, thank you, cousin. I've had more than sufficient.

COQUENARD. A banquet! Lucullus dines with Lucullus!

MME. COQUENARD. You must try my quince preserve, cousin.

PORTHOS. (*His teeth stuck with the fearsome dessert.*) Like a lamb to the slaughter . . .

MME. COQUENARD. I think I hear a carriage, husband. It must be the Doctor, come to bleed you. Albert!

COQUENARD. You must visit us again, cousin—if you survive the campaign. (*Albert supports him out.*)

MME. COQUENARD. Will you be in danger?

PORTHOS. Not if I'm well equipped. A fine charger. Saddle and harness. A valise. A new sword. Five hundred crowns should cover it.

MME. COQUENARD. Five hundred! It's a small fortune.

PORTHOS. Do you grudge that when my life depends on it? Remember what you vowed to me in Church.

MME. COQUENARD. Come, cousin Porthos. The key to the strong-box is in my bedroom. I believe it is time for my siesta.

PORTHOS. (*Seeing there is no alternative.*) Pour la France! (*He follows her out.*)

SCENE 29

Milady's chamber.
Milady and D'Artagnan come from bed.

MILADY. And now that I've given you proof of my love, D'Artagnan, you must satisfy me that I have yours. By tonight, the Comte must be dead.

D'ARTAGNAN. If you love me as much as you protest, aren't you afraid that I might be killed?

MILADY. That's impossible. With a swordsman like you?

D'ARTAGNAN. But suppose de Wardes isn't as guilty as you imagine.

MILADY. Explain yourself.

D'ARTAGNAN. I shall try—because I do have the assurance of your love, don't I?

MILADY. Completely. Go on.

D'ARTAGNAN. Well, my adorable mistress, I have a small confession to make. And now that I'm convinced of your love, I can dare to tell you. You kept an assignation with de Wardes two nights ago—in this very room.

MILADY. That isn't true.

D'ARTAGNAN. Don't lie, my angel. I was here. The Comte de Wardes of Thursday and the D'Artagnan of today are the same person. (*He attempts to embrace her, but Milady growls, and smashes D'Artagnan in the face. Grappling with her, D'Artagnan tears her night-dress, revealing the fleurs-de-lis on her shoulder.*)

The fleur-de-lis! (*Milady produces a dagger, D'Artagnan grabs his sword.*)

MILADY. You're the only man alive who knows my secret—and you'll die with it. (*She stabs and slashes. D'Artagnan holds her off.*) Scoundrel! Deceiver!

D'ARTAGNAN. Kitty!

KITTY. D'Artagnan! (*She brings his clothes, and he runs out with her. Milady tears her sheets.*)

SCENE 30

The Louvre.
The King and Cardinal review the troops. Musketeers emerge from one entrance and parade about, the Cardinal's Guards from the other, counter-marching. D'Artagnan runs across to emerge later more adequately dressed. The King, the Queen, the Cardinal are on the balcony. The troops present their battle standards for a blessing. The populace cheers and admires.

CARDINAL, GUARDS, & MUSKETEERS. Vivat! Vivat! Vivat! (*Cannons boom. Madame Coquenard, Kitty, attach themselves to Porthos, and D'Artagnan as the Musketeers leave: D'Artagnan is last in the line. Milady appears with two Bandits. She points him out to them, and they follow him off.*)

SCENE 31

La Rochefort: the Cardinal's headquarters. Cardinal, Rochefort and Jussac.

CARDINAL. Rochefort, I am assuming command of the siege. The essential is to bar the city to Buckingham's fleet. I propose to construct a dyke from here—to here; and so blockade the narrows.

ROCHEFORT. The Rochellais are an obstinate breed, your Eminence. The Mayor has hanged all those who advocate surrender.

CARDINAL. If they wish to die one by one of starvation, that is their affair. This is the last port in France open to the English; and defeat for the English means humiliation for Buckingham . . .

JUSSAC. (*At the entrance.*) M. D'Artagnan, your Eminence. (*D'Artagnan and Rochefort pass. D'Artagnan puts his hand to his sword, but lets it fall at the sight of the Cardinal.*)

CARDINAL. You are D'Artagnan—from Béarn in Gascony?

D'ARTAGNAN. Yes, your Eminence.

CARDINAL. The day after you were received by a great lady—whose valuable gift I note you preserve—I requested you call on me. You did not come.

D'ARTAGNAN. I feared I had incurred your displeasure, your Eminence.

CARDINAL. I punish those who disobey orders, not those who fulfill them. But I had a proposition to make you then, and I make it now. I have a vacancy for an ensign in my guards. You accept it?

D'ARTAGNAN. Your Eminence . . .

CARDINAL. You refuse?

D'ARTAGNAN. Your Eminence, my enemies, unhappily, are in your service. But my friends are in the Musketeers, and I hope one day to be worthy of a place beside them.

CARDINAL. So be it. But be vigilant, Monsieur, in the pursuit of your loves and hates. I have protected you until this moment.

D'ARTAGNAN. Your Eminence, so long as I act with honour, I ask you to remain neutral.

CARDINAL. Young man, if on a future occasion I am able to repeat the offer which I have made today—I say, if I am able—you have my word that I shall do so. (*D'Artagnan bows and leaves, troubled by the Cardinal's words.*) Jussac, has his Majesty arrived yet with the Musketeers?

JUSSAC. They are not expected before tomorrow, your Eminence.

CARDINAL. Very well. Confirm the arrangements for tonight. I will speak with our agent at ten, at the Red Dovecot.

SCENE 32

La Rochelle: out on patrol and D'Artagnan's tent.
As D'Artagnan patrols, he hears a click, and drops an instant before the shots. When the Bandits approach, he kills one and disarms the other.

D'ARTAGNAN. You're not a Rochellais! Then why did you try to kill me?

BANDIT. I was paid.

D'ARTAGNAN. Who employed you?

BANDIT. I don't know her name. There's a note in my belt.

D'ARTAGNAN. "After letting that woman slip through your fingers, make no mistake about the man. If you fail, I shall find you." Milady! What woman did you let slip through your fingers?

BANDIT. Some young woman we were guarding at Mantes jail. They jumped us one night, and took her off.

D'ARTAGNAN. So Constance is safe! My friend, I'm taking you back to camp.

BANDIT. To have me hanged?

D'ARTAGNAN. You deserve it. But you're brought me such wonderful news that I'll spare your life. You can help my servant instead. But first, tell me about the lady you were guarding. Was she well looked after? (*They leave for camp. Planchet comes on with a case of wine.*) And you heard the men say they were taking her to the Convent at Béthune?

BANDIT. That's what the old man in charge, M. Laporte, told them.

D'ARTAGNAN. M. Laporte! So the Queen's rescued Constance.

PLANCHET. Master, your friends have sent you a dozen bottles of chablis. The King's been delayed, and they knew you'd be missing their company, so they decided to cheer you up. Here's the letter.

D'ARTAGNAN. Why bother to seal it up again? What's your name, fellow?

BANDIT. Brisemont.

D'ARTAGNAN. Brisemont's agreed to help you, Planchet. Open the wine, Brisemont. Planchet, invite my companions. I'm going to drink to the Queen's health and to M. Laporte—and then to my beloved Constance. I'll count the hours till I can ride to Béthune. (*Planchet runs off. Brisemont opens a bottle and pours some—a mugful. He hands it to D'Artagnan. The sound of the Musketeers' singing is heard. D'Artagnan hands back the wine. Brisemont takes a swig as Athos, Porthos and Aramis enter.*) I was just about to try the wine you all sent me.

PORTHOS. What wine?

D'ARTAGNAN. The chablis.

ATHOS. I can see it's chablis, but it's nothing to do with us: we'd never give you anything less than champagne.

D'ARTAGNAN. But here's the letter.

ARAMIS. Not my writing—and certainly not my style. (*Brisemont shrieks and collapses.*)

BRISEMONT. You've killed me.

D'ARTAGNAN. Did you drink some?

BRISEMONT. Only a mouthful. Murderer! May God punish you. You pretend to forgive me, and then you poison me! (*Brisemont expires, groaning horribly.*)

D'ARTAGNAN. Milady meant that wine for me.

ATHOS. My friends, we seem to have acquired an additional enemy, and Milady de Winter is rather more formidable than the Rochellais. I propose we hold a council of war tonight, at the Red Dovecot.

D'ARTAGNAN. I'm on duty this evening.

ATHOS. Then we will have to meet without you. Get that corpse out of here. The dead make disagreeable company. (*Porthos and Aramis drag out the body. Planchet takes the wine, etc.*)

D'ARTAGNAN. Athos, you know that story you told me at Amiens, about a friend of yours and a girl he married—

ATHOS. You mustn't listen to me when I'm drunk. My imagination runs wild.

D'ARTAGNAN. But did your friend really hang that girl?

ATHOS. An extremely thorough hanging. Why do you ask?

D'ARTAGNAN. Because on her left shoulder, Milady has a fleur-de-lis. (*They go.*)

SCENE 33

The Red Dovecot.
Innkeeper comes in with bench. Three drunken soldiers follow him.

1ST. SOLDIER. We know there's a woman up there.

2ND. SOLDIER. Bring her down, and let's have a look at her.

3RD. SOLDIER. There's a man with her, and he's been there too long.

INNKEEPER. Messieurs, I beg you—

1ST. SOLDIER. Then we'll break the door in. (*Athos, Porthos, and Aramis arrive.*)

2ND. SOLDIER. There's a man upstairs with a whore—

INNKEEPER. She's not a whore, she's a lady.

PORTHOS. A lady! To the rescue. (*They have just routed the soldiers when two cloaked figures—the Cardinal and Jussac—appear.*)

CARDINAL. Jussac, arrest these men. I will not stand for this continual brawling.

ATHOS. Your Eminence! We fought to save a woman from three ruffians.

INNKEEPER. That's right, Your Eminence.

CARDINAL. What woman?

ATHOS. We haven't seen her. She's upstairs with a man, but as he didn't show his face, I presume he's not a gentleman.

CARDINAL. Judge not, that ye be not judged. Fetch the Comte, Jussac. Gentlemen, it appears there are undesirable characters about. It's important that I shouldn't be disturbed, so I'll ask you to remain here as my escort.

ROCHEFORT. Your Eminence. (*Rochefort bows to the Cardinal and goes out with Jussac.*)

CARDINAL. Bring some wine for these Musketeers. (*He goes upstairs.*)

ARAMIS. Have we rescued the Cardinal's mistress or something?

PORTHOS. After all, he's rather like you, Aramis: he's a soldier as well as a priest. (*To the Innkeeper.*) Have you got any dice? What about our council of war?

ATHOS. Sh! We'll talk about that later. (*Aramis and Porthos begin to play. Athos is leaning against a disused stovepipe, that stretches up to the balcony, on which the Cardinal and Milady appear.*)

CARDINAL. Milady, our situation is critical.

MILADY. Our situation?

CARDINAL. My situation, first. And yours, because you depend on me. La Rochelle will last indefinitely with help from England. And the King's patience will not. Something drastic must be done to stop the English fleet sailing.

MILADY. And what do you propose?

CARDINAL. There's a small boat waiting for you at the mouth of the Charente. Jussac will escort you there tonight. On the dawn tide, you will sail for Portsmouth. And soon I shall expect to hear about one of those strokes of fate which change the course of history.

MILADY. Assassination?

CARDINAL. Precisely.

MILADY. Would you send me to eternal damnation?

CARDINAL. You know I'm a man of God. But Buckingham has many enemies. It wouldn't be hard to find accomplices.

MILADY. My price would be high.

CARDINAL. Name it.

MILADY. First, my freedom from any further service. And the immediate possession of the Château de la Fère. Secondly, I demand the head of D'Artagnan.

CARDINAL. For what crime?

MILADY. I won't reveal what he has done to me. But I can provide ample evidence of his crimes against the state.

CARDINAL. Agreed, when I see the proof.

MILADY. Thirdly, I must have a carte blanche, signed by you, for what I'm about to attempt.

CARDINAL. Certainly. (*Athos leaves his listening post.*) "It is by my order and for the good of the State that the bearer of this paper has done what has been done. Richelieu."

PORTHOS. Athos!

ATHOS. Tell the Cardinal I'm patrolling ahead. I'll join you later. (*He hides.*)

CARDINAL. Jussac will be here shortly. When you get back to France send your report, and then go to the Convent at Béthune. Rochefort will meet you there. Milady, you hold our futures in your hands. I feel sure you won't let yourself down. And if you ever find life irksome in the seclusion of your Château, please get in touch with me. I can always find employment for you. (*He goes.*) Where's Athos?

PORTHOS. He's gone to reconnoitre the road back.

CARDINAL. And how have you passed the time?

ARAMIS. I won four crowns off Porthos.

CARDINAL. So. To horse, then, gentlemen. It's getting late. (*Porthos and Aramis leave with the Cardinal. As soon as they have gone, Athos slips out. Athos stands muffled in his cloak. Milady comes out.*)

ATHOS. Milady!

MILADY. Who are you?

ATHOS. Don't you remember?

MILADY. The Comte de la Fère!

ATHOS. The Comte de la Fère, risen from the grave for the pleasure of seeing you again. We believed each other dead, but Satan has resurrected you, though he cannot wash out the stains from your soul or the brand from your body. (*He seizes her, and bares her left shoulder.*) Anne de Breuil—that was your name when your brother married us. And yet you still want to play at being the Comtesse de la Fère.

MILADY. What do you want with me?

ATHOS. I want you to know that I've been watching you. I know that you stole two diamonds from Buckingham; that you had Constance Bonacieux abducted. That, hoping to pass the night adulterously with de Wardes, you instead entertained D'Artagnan. That you have twice attempted to kill him. And that as a reward for having Buckingham assassinated, you have asked for D'Artagnan's head.

MILADY. It's you who are Satan.

ATHOS. Perhaps. But listen to me all the same. Buckingham doesn't concern me. He's an Englishman. But D'Artagnan is my friend. And I swear that if you harm one hair of his head, it will be the last crime you live to commit.

MILADY. He insulted me, and he'll die for it.

ATHOS. Can a thing like you be insulted?

MILADY. He'll die first, and that woman of his afterwards. (*Athos draws his pistol, and aims it at her head.*)

ATHOS. Give me that paper from the Cardinal, or I'll blow your brains out. You have three seconds.

MILADY. Take it, and my curse. (*She spits at him, and tries to bite him.*)

ATHOS. You viper; but your fangs are drawn.

JUSSAC. (*Outside.*) Landlord!

ATHOS. Milady is ready. You know the Cardinal's orders. (*He goes.*)

JUSSAC. Milady! Your ship is waiting. (*He escorts Milady out.*)

SCENE 34

La Rochelle: D'Artagnan's tent. Aramis, Porthos, D'Artagnan.

ARAMIS. Such a charming lady—having failed to have you shot and poisoned, my dear fellow, she has demanded your head from the Cardinal. (*Athos enters.*)

ATHOS. She has sailed for England. Let us ensure that she stays there. She has a brother—

PORTHOS. And how should we inform him? We cannot take ship to Portsmouth.

D'ARTAGNAN. I would answer for Planchet. But I shall not feel happy until Constance is in my care. How shall we discover where the Queen has hidden her?

ARAMIS. I know a person in Tours who will do that.

ATHOS. And I will answer for Grimaud.

D'ARTAGNAN. Then Aramis must write the letters. Suggest to Lord de Winter that he questions Milady about her first husband.

ATHOS. And tell him, if he requires proof, he will find her past written on her left shoulder. (*Aramis writes.*)

D'ARTAGNAN. Planchet! (*Planchet appears.*) Planchet, we are going to present you with the chance of a lifetime. You can win yourself two hundred crowns, and cover yourself with glory.

PLANCHET. Glory, Monsieur? I prefer the crowns.

D'ARTAGNAN. It's eight o'clock. You have eight days to reach Portsmouth, where you will seek an interview with Lord de Winter. You will give him this letter. You have eight days to return. And if you arrive so much as one minute later than eight o'clock—no crowns.

PLANCHET. Then you must buy me a watch, Monsieur.

ATHOS. Take mine. And Planchet—guard your tongue. If evil should happen to your master through any fault of yours, I will find you, Planchet. And when I have found you, I will slit open your belly.

PLANCHET. Yes, Monsieur.

PORTHOS. And I will flay your hide off.

ARAMIS. And I will roast you on a spit.

PLANCHET. Oh, Messieurs, I promise you—I will succeed.

SCENE 35

Lord de Winter's castle.
Planchet gives a letter to Lord de Winter. Then Milady
is brought in with an English Guard, and Felton.

MILADY. I demand an explanation. My ship was delayed ten days, and my business is urgent. Why have you brought me here from Portsmouth?

FELTON. I am acting under orders, Madame. (*Lord de Winter enters.*)

MILADY. Brother!

LORD DE WINTER. Welcome to England, sister.

MILADY. Is this your castle?

LORD DE WINTER. It is.

MILADY. But I've been treated like a prisoner, not a guest.

LORD DE WINTER. That will soon be settled. Leave us, John. (*Felton goes.*) Isn't this place sufficiently luxurious for you?

MILADY. Yes.

LORD DE WINTER. Tell me how your first husband looked after you, and I'll do my best to emulate him.

MILADY. My first husband?

LORD DE WINTER. The Comte de la Fère.

MILADY. You're drunk, or mad. (*She springs at him.*)

LORD DE WINTER. I've no scruples about defending myself.

MILADY. Yes, you would be the sort to hit a woman.

LORD DE WINTER. It won't be the first time a man has left his mark on you. (*He points to her shoulder. She growls.*)

MILADY. Fool. Imbecile.

LORD DE WINTER. Spit and snarl as much as you please. I see all my suspicions are confirmed. You bigamous reptile, sliding between my brother's sheets—and I suppose you were responsible for his death. I know judges who would try you tonight, brand your other shoulder and send you to Tyburn. But I'll be merciful. In a week we leave for La Rochelle. And the evening before we sail, you'll sail for another destination: the penal colony in America. John—come in, my dear fellow. Be on your guard with this woman. She looks young and beautiful. But inside, she's rotten and corrupt. She may try to seduce you, John. But I know your Puritan virtues will arm you against the temptations of the flesh. (*He goes. Felton remains at a distance. Milady collapses temporarily.*)

MILADY. You won't stop me praying to my Redeemer?

FELTON. God forbid I should prevent a sinner from asking for forgiveness.

MILADY. More sinned against than sinning. O God above, thou alone knowest our inmost thoughts: have mercy upon me. Put not your trust in princes, nor in any son of man, for there is no help in them. (*She starts to chant.*)

FELTON. Guard!

MILADY. Out of the deep have I called unto thee, O Lord. Lord, hear my voice. (*The Guard escorts her off. Felton is visibly moved by this angelic sinner.*)

SCENE 36

The Queen appears with Laporte. She is writing a letter.

QUEEN. "My lord, I write this as a last appeal. If you know that every hurt done to France wounds me equally, I cannot believe that you will lead your invasion fleet out of harbour. Because of you men's lives have been endangered; because of you Constance Bonacieux has sought refuge in a Convent. I am sending you my diamonds. You accepted them once as a pledge of peace; I pray that no more innocent blood will be spilt." (*She signs her name.*) "Anne of Austria." Laporte, I have made arrangements for your journey to Portsmouth. Give these diamonds, and this letter, to the Duke of Buckingham. And if he hesitates to act—tell him that I love him.

SCENE 37

Lord de Winter's castle.
Milady is in her nightdress. She is shackled. A Guard is
with her. Felton enters.

FELTON. This last hour I'll keep guard in your place.
GUARD. I envy you, Lieutenant Felton. (*He goes.*)
FELTON. Tell me when Lord de Winter comes. (*He approaches Milady.*) I promised and here I am.
MILADY. Felton, find me someone I can pour out my soul to. There is no one here of the Puritan faith who can understand my suffering.
FELTON. Then we share the same faith?
MILADY. Felton, I didn't realize. Thank God. Then I can tell you a secret I've never dared confide to any man. I know you won't hear a word against Lord de Winter. But let me tell you about the man who has corrupted him. The man for whose lust you are guarding me.
FELTON. God forbid!
MILADY. God may forbid in vain, while men like him rule the country. Felton, three years ago at a great ball a man asked me to give him—what it would have been mortal sin to give. But because he obeys no laws of God or man, he came to my bed at night. I cried out. I struggled. I clawed at his flesh with my nails. But he laughed at me. He said: "I don't have much use for Puritans. But pretty little Puritan girls amuse me." He placed a wet sponge over my mouth. And although I gasped and spat, I couldn't prevent a few drops trickling down my throat. I fainted. When I woke up, I was in a strange room, sprawled naked on a gold bed among silk sheets and pillows. And as I opened my eyes, a mocking voice rang in my ears. "Ah, my dear, you may resist me when you're awake, but you should see what you do in your sleep."
FELTON. Who was it?

73

MILADY. He kept me prisoner for a week. And every night he forced himself on me. I would have killed myself, but I was never allowed a knife.

FELTON. Who was he?

MILADY. Eventually, my guard took pity on me, and carried me to safety. Safety! Nowhere in the world was I safe from that monster's lust and cruelty. One night two masked men broke into my apartment. They stripped and bound me. I was thrown on the floor. And one of them said, in a voice I knew so well, "You're a prostitute, and you'll be punished as a prostitute. Executioner, do your duty." And the red-hot iron was plunged onto my shoulder, till I screamed from the pain and fainted from the stench of burning flesh. Look at my left shoulder, Felton, and see how this country rewards chastity. (*Felton bears her shoulder.*)

FELTON. The fleur-de-lis!

MILADY. The mark of England would require a court of law. But who would question the mark of France? (*Felton is overwhelmed. He kisses her shoulder, and falls at her feet.*)

FELTON. Forgive me! O God, forgive me!

MILADY. For what?

FELTON. For having joined your persecutors. Tell me his name, so that I can avenge you.

MILADY. Who else but Antichrist himself?

FELTON. Buckingham.

GUARD. (*Outside.*) Lord de Winter, sir. (*De Winter enters.*)

LORD DE WINTER. The carriage is ready, John. These are the papers—they only need the Duke of Buckingham's signature. I'll join you at his headquarters. Bon voyage, sister. I think this promises to be your last and longest journey. (*He leaves. Felton hesitates, then unshackles Milady. He takes her in his arms, kisses her, and runs out with her.*)

SCENE 38

Buckingham's flagship.
Buckingham is just out of the bath. Patrick enters.

PATRICK. Lieutenant Felton from Lord de Winter.

74

BUCKINGHAM. Show him in. Why didn't Lord de Winter come himself?

FELTON. He had to make some arrangements about the prisoner. I'd like to discuss her with you, my lord—privately.

BUCKINGHAM. Oh, very well. Patrick, leave us for a minute. (*Patrick goes.*)

FELTON. My lord, this is the order for Milady de Winter's transportation.

BUCKINGHAM. Well, give it here, and I'll sign it.

FELTON. Can you do that without remorse?

BUCKINGHAM. What an extraordinary question.

FELTON. Reply to it, my lord. The circumstances are more serious than you imagine.

BUCKINGHAM. Without remorse. As Lord de Winter knows, Milady is guilty of many crimes, and transportation is a lenient punishment.

FELTON. You will never sign that order, my lord. But I insist you sign this—a free pardon.

BUCKINGHAM. Mr. Felton, you will withdraw at once. Consider yourself under arrest.

FELTON. You will hear me out. You seduced this innocent girl. You defiled the pure temple of her body. You are held in horror by God and man. But let her go free, and I will spare you.

BUCKINGHAM. I'll have you court-martialled.

FELTON. Sign.

BUCKINGHAM. Never. Patrick! Help! (*Felton stabs him. Patrick and a Guard run in and overpower him, followed by Lord de Winter.*)

LORD DE WINTER. Your Grace!

BUCKINGHAM. Is that you, de Winter? You sent a strange fellow to see me this morning.

LORD DE WINTER. Felton.

BUCKINGHAM. See what he has done to me.

LORD DE WINTER. I shall never forgive myself. (*Laporte enters.*)

BUCKINGHAM. My dear de Winter, I don't deserve a lifetime's regret. Laporte! A letter from—her?

LAPORTE. A letter, my lord—and this. (*He gives Buckingham the diamonds and letter.*)

LORD DE WINTER. John, did the devil possess you?

FELTON. Not the devil—an angel. (*A ship's bell: he looks out of the window.*) But that's our ship. She didn't wait for me.

LORD DE WINTER. John, you'll be punished for the crime your hand committed. But I swear that the woman who guided it will not go free.

BUCKINGHAM. Patrick! Cancel the orders for the fleet.

PATRICK. Yes, my lord.

BUCKINGHAM. The expedition will not sail. Laporte, restore these diamonds to the Queen. Tell her that I obeyed her with my final breath. Tell her that my eyes closed looking on her treasure. Tell her I died, not for England, but for France. And—give her this. (*He takes the dagger out of his side, kisses it, and dies.*)

SCENE 39

The convent at Béthune.
The Abbess and Milady.

ABBESS. We'll do our best to make you comfortable, Madame. Those were the Cardinal's orders.

MILADY. I wish I could believe his real intentions towards me are so considerate.

ABBESS. But Madame, I thought you were one of his friends . . .

MILADY. One of his victims.

ABBESS. How can a lady such as you have possibly offended him?

MILADY. There are some virtues the Cardinal punishes more severely than offences.

ABBESS. Poor Madame, I understand now—and that makes you my second refugee.

MILADY. Who else are you sheltering here?

ABBESS. Such a sweet young lady—they called her Kitty. She's been involved in some intrigue at Court.

MILADY. Could I see her? I feel such sympathy for her.

ABBESS. Certainly, Madame. I'll fetch her now. (*She goes.*)

MILADY. Can this be my Kitty? I'll tear her eyes out. (*The door opens, and Constance appears, dressed as a nun.*)

CONSTANCE. Madame, the Abbess said you'd like to see me.

MILADY. My dear, I thought you might be lonely; we could help each other pass the time.

CONSTANCE. Oh, if only you'd come sooner. I've been here on my own for three weeks. And now you've arrived just as I'm about to leave.

MILADY. You're going soon?

CONSTANCE. I hope and pray I am. I had this note yesterday, to say my friends would soon be in Paris, and then they'd come straight here.

MILADY. And who are these gallant friends?

CONSTANCE. Perhaps you know them, Madame: you must know so many people in Paris. They're Musketeers—Aramis, Porthos, Athos and—

MILADY. Athos!

CONSTANCE. You know him?

MILADY. I know of him—through a friend of his, D'Artagnan.

CONSTANCE. D'Artagnan! You know him too? Excuse me, Madame, but in what capacity do you know him?

MILADY. Why, as a friend.

CONSTANCE. You're not speaking the truth. You've been his mistress.

MILADY. No, you're the mistress. I know you now—you're Constance Bonacieux! Don't deny it.

CONSTANCE. I am, Madame. But—are we rivals?

MILADY. The last thing in the world, my dear. But surely the Musketeers are at La Rochelle?

CONSTANCE. They should be. But nothing's impossible for my D'Artagnan. (*A horse is heard.*) Can this be him? (*She leaps to the window.*)

MILADY. Can you see him?

CONSTANCE. I can't tell. He's gone inside.

MILADY. It must be a visitor for one of us.

CONSTANCE. How pale you look. (*The Abbess enters.*)

ABBESS. A gentleman to see the Lady from Boulogne.

CONSTANCE. It's for you, Madame. I'll retire.

MILADY. Thank you, Constance. But come back to see me the moment he's gone.

CONSTANCE. Oh, I will, I will. (*She goes.*)

77

MILADY. Ask him to come in.

ABBESS. Certainly, Madame. Come this way, please. (*Rochefort enters. Milady gives a cry of relief.*)

MILADY. My brave Chevalier, it's you.

ROCHEFORT. As charming as ever, Milady. The Cardinal received your message, but he sent me to find out the details.

MILADY. I've no details to give him. Buckingham is dead or wounded. The fleet has not sailed. If I'd stayed to enquire further, I wouldn't have reached Boulogne.

ROCHEFORT. When did you arrive?

MILADY. This morning. And I haven't wasted my time. The little Bonacieux woman is next door. She expects to be joined any day now by D'Artagnan and his friends. I can't stay here.

ROCHEFORT. Unfortunately, I have the strictest orders to collect your despatches and return to the Cardinal.

MILADY. Then take me with you.

ROCHEFORT. Impossible, I'm afraid. The Cardinal has ordered you to stay here, and wait for instructions about the Château de la Fère.

MILADY. And what if the Musketeers come?

ROCHEFORT. I'm sure you are more than capable of dealing with them. You must hide in the neighbourhood. I suppose I could leave my spare horse for you.

MILADY. There's a road behind that wood. I can reach it through the gardens. Tether him there—and send help the moment you can.

ROCHEFORT. Anything to please you, Milady— I'll take him there at once.

MILADY. Adieu, Chevalier. Remember me to his Eminence.

ROCHEFORT. Adieu, Belle Dame Sans Merci— Remember me to Satan. (*Rochefort leaves. A knock on the door and Constance comes in.*)

CONSTANCE. Who was that man, Madame?

MILADY. My brother. The Cardinal's men are on their way. He was at an inn nearby and he overheard them plotting how to capture us. He says they may be here within the hour.

CONSTANCE. What shall we do?

MILADY. He'll wait for us in the wood beyond the garden. (*A horse goes by.*) There he goes now. In a few minutes we'll slip out and join him.

CONSTANCE. But how will D'Artagnan find me?

MILADY. We'll hide in the neighbourhood. And every day my brother can ride to the village, until your friends arrive. Now, go and collect your things. (*A noise of horses is heard, and shouts. Constance goes white.*)

CONSTANCE. What is it?

MILADY. (*Looking out of the window.*) The Cardinal's Guards. Come on, my dear, we still have time—

CONSTANCE. My strength's gone—I can't move.

MILADY. For the last time, will you follow me?

CONSTANCE. You must go alone. Leave me here. (*Milady runs to the table, and pours some wine into a glass. She empties a powder into it.*)

MILADY. Here, drink this. The wine will give you strength. (*Constance obeys her. Milady rushes out. Constance remains motionless. Gradually she moves over to lean on the table. From outside, she can hear footsteps—and D'Artagnan's voice.*)

D'ARTAGNAN. Mother Superior, have you a young woman here called Constance Bonacieux?

CONSTANCE. D'Artagnan! D'Artagnan! Is it really you? I'm here, I'm here!

D'ARTAGNAN. Constance! (*The Musketeers burst in. D'Artagnan takes Constance in his arms.*)

CONSTANCE. Oh my beloved D'Artagnan, you've come at last. I knew it, though she tried to persuade me you wouldn't!

ATHOS. She? Who's she?

CONSTANCE. My companion. She thought you were the Cardinal's Guards, and wanted me to escape with her.

D'ARTAGNAN. But her name! What's her name?

CONSTANCE. The Abbess did tell me. I feel so faint. (*Aramis sees the glass of wine.*)

ARAMIS. Who poured you this glass of wine?

CONSTANCE. She did.

PORTHOS. Who is she?

CONSTANCE. Oh, I remember. Milady de Winter. (*She collapses again in the arms of Porthos and Aramis. D'Artagnan turns to Athos.*)

D'ARTAGNAN. No! O, God!

ATHOS. All things are possible with her.

CONSTANCE. D'Artagnan! D'Artagnan! Where are you? Don't leave me. I'm dying.

D'ARTAGNAN. Aramis, Porthos, run for help.

ATHOS. There's no antidote for the poison she pours.

CONSTANCE. Ah, my love, it's true. D'Artagnan. (*She kisses D'Artagnan and dies.*)

D'ARTAGNAN. Constance— (*He falls by her side. Porthos weeps. Aramis prays. Athos makes the sign of the cross. Lord de Winter appears.*)

LORD DE WINTER. I see she has been before us. Are they both dead?

ATHOS. No, only Constance. My friend, remember who you are. Women weep for the dead. Men avenge them.

D'ARTAGNAN. Oh, if we're to avenge her, I am with you.

PORTHOS. Let's ride after her.

ATHOS. There will be time enough. First, we must see this innocent child buried. Then you will all go to the inn. I have some plans to make. The servants can track her down. (*The Abbess enters.*)

D'ARTAGNAN. Constance!

ATHOS. Treat her as one of your order. Let her Requiem be sung in the chapel tonight. (*They carry out the body.*)

LORD DE WINTER. I feel I should be in charge of the plans from now on. After all, Milady is my sister-in-law.

ATHOS. Lord de Winter, she happens to be my wife.

SCENE 40

The riverbank—night.
Planchet is on watch. Milady passes, followed by Grimaud. Then come the four Musketeers, de Winter and a cloaked man.

PORTHOS. Who is that man?

ATHOS. Be patient. D'Artagnan, not so fast. (*A low whistle from Planchet.*)

D'ARTAGNAN. Have you lost her?

PLANCHET. No, sir. She's very close—by the river. Grimaud's watching her.

ATHOS. Lead on. (*They go off. Milady returns, followed by Grimaud. When the others appear, Grimaud gestures towards her, D'Artagnan and the others surround and confront her. D'Artagnan draws his pistol, but Athos restrains him.*) Put that down. This creature must be tried, not assassinated. Come forward, gentlemen.

MILADY. What do you want?

ATHOS. We want Anne de Brieul, later known as the Comtesse de la Fère, and afterwards as Milady de Winter.

MILADY. I am she. But what do you want with me?

ATHOS. We wish to judge your crimes. You're at liberty to defend yourself, if you can. M. D'Artagnan, you must make the first accusation.

D'ARTAGNAN. Before God and before men, I accuse this woman of poisoning Constance Bonacieux, who died yesterday.

PORTHOS & ARAMIS. We bear witness to this.

D'ARTAGNAN. I accuse her of hiring two men to murder me. One of them died in the attempt, the other was poisoned by wine meant for me.

PORTHOS & ARAMIS. We bear witness to this.

ATHOS. Your turn, my lord.

LORD DE WINTER. Before God and before men, I accuse this woman of causing the assassination of the Duke of Buckingham. I accuse her of corrupting my loyal servant, John Felton, who is even now paying with his head for the crime she urged him to commit. That is not all. My brother died within an hour of an agonizing disease that tore his body. Woman, how did my brother die?

ATHOS. Now it is my turn. I married that woman when she was a young girl. I gave her my love, my wealth and my name. And then I discovered that, on her left shoulder, she had been branded with the fleur-de-lis.

MILADY. I defy you to name the court which passed that sentence. I defy you to find the man who executed it.

EXECUTIONER. Silence! It is for me to reply.

MILADY. Who is that man? No, no, it's a ghost.

ALL. Who are you?

EXECUTIONER. Ask the woman.

MILADY. The executioner of Lille.

EXECUTIONER. That woman was once in a convent where a young priest took confession. She seduced him—she would have seduced a saint. She persuaded him to run away with her, and in order to have enough money, she made him steal the holy vessels from the Church. They were arrested, imprisoned, branded. I carried out the sentence. A year later they escaped, and fled to Berry, where the Lord of the estate saw her, and fell in love with her. She left the priest who had sold his soul for her, and became the Comtesse de la Fère. The priest hanged himself. That priest was my brother. This is the crime I accuse her of.

ATHOS. M. D'Artagnan, what penalty do you demand for this woman?

D'ARTAGNAN. Death.

ATHOS. My Lord de Winter, what penalty do you demand for this woman?

LORD DE WINTER. Death.

ATHOS. Messieurs Porthos and Aramis, in your capacity as impartial judges, what sentence do you pronounce on this woman?

ARAMIS & PORTHOS. The sentence of death.

ATHOS. Anne de Brieul, Comtesse de la Fère, Milady de Winter. Your crimes have wearied men on earth and God in heaven. If you know a prayer, this is the time to say it. For you have been condemned, and you must die. Grimaud, lead her to the river. (*He escorts her. The others follow.*)

MILADY. (*Whispering.*) A thousand crowns for you, if you help me escape. If you refuse, I've friends who will revenge me.

LORD DE WINTER. Change that servant. I saw her speak to him.

ATHOS. Planchet! (*Planchet takes Grimaud's place.*)

MILADY. Cowards! Eight men to murder one woman. I may not be saved, but I shall be avenged. The Cardinal will see to that.

ATHOS. You forget we have his permission. (*He reads the carte blanche.*) "It is by my order and for the good of the state that the bearer of this paper has done what has been done."

MILADY. Then remember, whoever kills me is a murderer.

EXECUTIONER. But the executioner may kill without being named a murderer. And here I have the last judge. (*He produces the axe.*)

MILADY. Have pity on me. I'm so young.

ARAMIS. Constance Bonacieux was younger than you.

MILADY. O God, O God, are all your hearts so cold?

D'ARTAGNAN. We mustn't let her die like this.

MILADY. D'Artagnan, remember our night together; how we loved each other, how I held you in my arms! (*D'Artagnan takes a step towards her.*)

ATHOS. One step more, D'Artagnan, and I run you through. Executioner, do your duty.

EXECUTIONER. Willingly.

ATHOS. I forgive you the harm you've done me. I forgive you for my bitter youth, my stained honour, my warped love. Die in peace.

LORD DE WINTER. I forgive you for the murder of my brother, for the corruption of John Felton, for the assassination of the Duke of Buckingham. Die in peace.

D'ARTAGNAN. Forgive me, Milady, for provoking your anger by my deception. And in return, I forgive you for the cruel murder of my innocent love. I shall weep for you. Die in peace.

MILADY. So I have reached the end. Is this the place?

EXECUTIONER. It is. On your knees.

ATHOS. Here is your fee, so she may know we act as judges.

EXECUTIONER. That is in order. And now, let this woman see that I am fulfilling, not my profession, but my duty. (*He throws the money in the river. He raises his axe, and lets it fall.*) May the Justice of God be done!

SCENE 41

Paris: various locations.
The Cardinal is seated at his desk. Jussac brings in D'Artagnan.

CARDINAL. Monsieur, you have been arrested at my orders. The charge laid against you is conspiracy: conspiracy with the enemies of the state; conspiracy against your sovereign; conspiracy against your commanding officer.

D'ARTAGNAN. And who lays these charges, Monseigneur? A

woman branded by the justice of her country, a woman who married one man in France and another in England, who poisoned her second husband, who has attempted both to poison and assassinate me.

CARDINAL. What woman do you speak of?

D'ARTAGNAN. Milady de Winter.

CARDINAL. If Milady de Winter has committed such crimes, she will be punished.

D'ARTAGNAN. She has been punished. She is dead.

CARDINAL. By whose hand?

D'ARTAGNAN. My friends and I tried her, and condemned her to death.

CARDINAL. Those who punish without licence are assassins under the law. I can tell you now that you too will be tried and condemned to death.

D'ARTAGNAN. Monseigneur, I have a carte blanche.

CARDINAL. Signed by the King?

D'ARTAGNAN. (*He hands it over.*) Signed by yourself, Monseigneur.

CARDINAL. "It is by my order and for the good of the state that the bearer of this paper has done what has been done." (*The Cardinal is silent a moment. He looks at D'Artagnan. He tears up the carte blanche. He writes a line on another parchment, and affixes his seal.*) Monsieur, I have taken one carte blanche from you. I give you another. It is a lieutenant's commission in the Musketeers.

D'ARTAGNAN. (*He falls on his knees.*) Your Eminence, my life stands at your disposal. But this is an honour I don't deserve. I have three friends—

CARDINAL. Do what you wish with the commission, D'Artagnan. But remember, I give it to you. Rochefort! (*Rochefort enters.*) Rochefort. You have met M. D'Artagnan before, I believe. From today, I number him among my friends. Greet each other. (*They bow to each other, to the Cardinal, and withdraw.*)

ROCHEFORT. We shall meet again, no doubt, Monsieur.

D'ARTAGNAN. Whenever you please. (*The Cardinal and Rochefort go. D'Artagnan meets Athos. Athos is drinking the last of the wine.*) Here, Athos—this should be yours. (*Hands him the commission.*)

ATHOS. My friend—for Athos, this is too much. For the Comte de la Fère, too little. Keep it. You have paid dearly for it. (*D'Artagnan goes to Porthos, who is parading a new costume in front of a mirror.*)
PORTHOS. How do my new clothes fit me?
D'ARTAGNAN. Magnificently. But I have come to offer you an even more splendid uniform. A lieutenancy in the Musketeers. Write your name here.
PORTHOS. You flatter me, D'Artagnan. But I should not have time to attend to my duties. During our campaign my Duchess buried her husband. The strong-box beckons, and these are my wedding garments. (*D'Artagnan leaves Porthos, and finds Aramis, at prayer.*)
D'ARTAGNAN. Aramis, take this. You have deserved it by the wisdom of your counsel.
ARAMIS. Alas, D'Artagnan. Our recent adventures have soured the soldier's life for me, and even my lady of Tours could not make me change my mind. I shall enter the order of the Jesuits. The profession of arms suits you, my dear friend. Keep the commission. (*D'Artagnan leaves Aramis and returns to Athos.*)
D'ARTAGNAN. They too have refused me.
ATHOS. And that is because no-one is more worthy than you, my friend. Here (*He takes the commission.*)— I will write your name myself.
D'ARTAGNAN. And my friends will be no more. I shall have nothing but bitter memories.
ATHOS. You are young, D'Artagnan. Your bitter memories will sweeten with time.

CURTAIN

PRODUCTION NOTE

This adaptation, although ideal for a large company with opportunities for colourful crowd scenes, has also been successfully performed with a cast of 25 (20m, 5f). Some of the possibilities for doubling are set out below.

The main staging requirement is for two levels, with perhaps the addition of a trap-door, or the suggestion of one. D'Artagnan's apartment (scene 8) is above Bonacieux's shop (scenes 10 and 12), and ideally there should be access between the two; the Red Dovecot (scene 33) also needs two levels. Several other scenes (such as 4, 19, 20, 27) would benefit from such an arrangement. In scenes 15 and 23, Athos and Grimaud spend some time in the inn's cellar. A design that incorporates multiple levels, with a balcony and flights of stairs, would give plenty of scope for lively chases and fights.

The play works best if it moves fast, giving the impression of a film, with cuts and dissolves. Generally, one scene should flow into the next with the minimum of delay. The locations should be defined by imaginative sound effects and selected props, rather than by elaborate settings. Devices such as reversible inn-signs, sign-posts etc. would be appropriate.

The following "doubles" can be achieved:
D'Artagnan's Father, Buckingham, Executioner
D'Artagnan's Mother, Anne of Austria
Jussac, Musketeer's Sergeant
De Tréville, Innkeeper at Jolly Miller—Shoulder of Mutton—Red Dovecot
Bonacieux, O'Reilly, Lord de Winter
Coquenard, Laporte
Mme. Coquenard, Landlady at Amiens
1st. Musketeer, Cardinal's Guard, Stranger, Guard at Amiens, Drunken Soldier
2nd. Musketeer, Cardinal's Guard, Workman, Patrick, Beggar, Drunken Soldier
3rd. Musketeer, Cardinal's Guard, Workman, Ormsby, Bandit, Drunken Soldier
4th. Musketeer, Guard at Louvre, Guard at Amiens, Apprentice, Bandit, English Guard

King, Sea-Captain, Jesuit
Constance, Kitty
Dona Estefania, Abbess
Comte de Wardes, Curé, Felton
Musketeer, Grimaud
Musketeer, Planchet
The other parts are:
D'Artagnan; Rochefort; Bicarat; Milady de Winter; Porthos; Aramis; Athos; the Cardinal

NOTES ON THE CHIEF CHARACTERS

The Musketeers:

M. DE TRÉVILLE: the elderly Captain of the King's Musketeers, extremely jealous of their reputation.

D'ARTAGNAN: a young Gascon, dashing, romantic, impetuous.

PORTHOS: in his mid-twenties; muscular, loud-mouthed, vain. A follower of Mme. Coquenard, his 'Duchess'.

ARAMIS: poetic, spiritual, in love with the absent Mme. de Chevreuse. In his late twenties.

ATHOS: older than the others, more withdrawn, and scarred by his unhappy past. As the Comte de la Fère, once married to Milady.

GRIMAUD: Athos' servant. Entirely silent.

PLANCHET: D'Artagnan's servant. A realist.

The Court:

KING LOUIS XIII: rather effete—an ineffectual ruler who relies heavily on the Cardinal, though he supports the private quarrels of his Musketeers against the Cardinal's Guards.

QUEEN ANNE: of Austria. In love with Buckingham, and an enemy of the Cardinal, though loyal to France and the King.

LAPORTE: her devoted valet.

DONA ESTEFANIA: her lady-in-waiting—in the Cardinal's pay.

CONSTANCE BONACIEUX: young and pretty, the Queen's trusted lady-in-waiting. An admirer of D'Artagnan.

The Cardinal's party:

CARDINAL RICHELIEU: Chief Minister of France, devious and formidable.

COMTE DE ROCHEFORT: his right-hand man; unsmiling—'tall and dark, with a scar on his left temple'.

JUSSAC, BICARAT: Lieutenants in the Cardinal's Guards.

MILADY DE WINTER: a blonde femme fatale in the Cardinal's service. Formerly married to the Comte de la Fère. Attracted to the Comte de Wardes.

COMTE DE WARDES: a young nobleman.

KITTY: Milady's pretty maid, who falls instantly in love with D'Artagnan.

The English:

DUKE OF BUCKINGHAM: Chief Minister of England, with a reputation for ruthlessness and godlessness. Obsessively in love with Anne of Austria.

LORD DE WINTER: brother of a former husband of Milady's. A sincere but not very intelligent English peer.

FELTON: a young Lieutenant, and protégé of de Winter's. An impressionable Puritan.

The Parisians:

M. BONACIEUX: a grocer. The miserly, elderly, suspicious husband of Constance, and D'Artagnan's landlord.

M. COQUENARD: a tight-fisted and decrepit lawyer, husband to Mme. Coquenard.

MME. COQUENARD: a scrawny middle-aged woman, in love with Porthos.

LIST OF PROPERTIES AND ESSENTIAL FURNITURE

ACT ONE

Scene:

1. Purse, with coins (Father)
   Letter (Father)
   Sword (Father)
   Recipe (Mother)
   Bundle (D'Artagnan)
2. Wine and glasses
   Table, stools
   Fire-tongs, shovel
   Coins (Bicarat)
3. Onions, tomatoes (Bonacieux)
   Coins (Coquenard, Mme. Coquenard)
   Bundle (D'Artagnan, as in 1)
4. Poem book, pen (Aramis)
   Lace handkerchief (cloaked figure)
   Handkerchief (Aramis)
   Sling for wound (Athos)
5. Breakable sword (Bicarat)
   Note (Mme. Coquenard)
6. Bag of gold (King)
7. Diamonds (Queen)
8. Breviary, poem-book (Aramis)
   Table, stools
   Wine, glasses, food
9. Hand bell
   Desk, chair
   Pigeon with message (Bicarat)
10. Boot brush (Planchet)
    Large cheese, other goods for shop
    Paper, pen (Constance)
11. Chess board and men
    Table, 2 chairs
    Letter (Queen)
    Note (Guard)
12. Letter (D'Artagnan)
    Moneychest, money bags

Keys (Constance)
Note (Athos)
13. Pigeon (Innkeeper)
Table, stools
Wine, tankards
14. Planks for bridge
Workmen's implements
Muskets (Workmen)
15. Pigeon and note (Landlady)
Money (Athos)
Pistols (Athos)
16. Diamonds (Buckingham—as in 7)
Scissors (Milady)
17. Permit (de Wardes)
18. Altar, with portrait of Queen, and diamonds
Letter (D'Artagnan)
Jeweller's instruments (O'Reilly)
19. Diamonds (Queen)
Packet with 2 diamonds in it (Milady)
Ring (Queen)

Act Two

Scene:
20. Ring (D'Artagnan—as in 19)
21. Wheel-chair (Porthos)
Bill (Porthos)
22. Theological books
Table, 3 stools
Letter (D'Artagnan)
Dish of spinach (Planchet)
23. Wine, glasses, ham
Pistols (D'Artagnan, Planchet)
Card (de Winter)
24. 2 notes (Kitty)
2 chairs
26. Candelabra
Ring (Milady)
27. Handkerchief (Aramis)
Letter (Beggar)
Gold coins (Beggar)
Ring (D'Artagnan—as in 26)
Paper, pen (D'Artagnan)

90

28. Meal—chicken, quince preserve, wine, water, etc.
    Table, 3 chairs
    Bed
29. Dagger (Milady)
    Sheets
30. Battle standards
31. Ring (D'Artagnan—as in 19)
32. Muskets (Bandits)
    Note (2nd Bandit)
    Case of wine (Planchet)
    Mug
33. Wine, glasses
    Table, 2 stools
    Dice (Innkeeper)
    Paper, pen (Cardinal)
    Pistol (Athos)
34. Paper, pen (Aramis)
    Watch (Athos)
35. Letter (Planchet)
36. Paper, pen (Queen)
    Diamonds (Queen)
37. Shackles (Milady)
    Key (Felton)
    Papers (de Winter)
38. Papers (Felton)
    Dagger (Felton)
    Letter, diamonds (Laporte—as in 36)
39. Wine and glasses
    Table, 2 chairs
    Poison (Milady)
40. Axe (Executioner)
    Pistol (D'Artagnan)
    Carte blanche (Athos)
    Money (Athos)
41. Carte blanche (D'Artagnan)
    Desk, chair
    Parchment, pen (Cardinal)
    Wine (Athos)
    Breviary (Aramis)
    Pen (Athos)

Swords: swords are usually worn, and needed, by:
   D'Artagnan (who receives his father's); Rochefort; Jussac; Bicarat;
   Musketeers; Porthos; Aramis; Athos; de Tréville; de Wardes;
   Ormsby; de Winter

SOUND EFFECTS

Scene:
1. Horse neighing
   Horse hooves
2. Horse hooves—someone dismounting
3. Street noises
5. Clock striking twelve
14. Water lapping
16. Music—state ball
17. Harbour noises
19. Fanfares
   Stately dance
23. Banging, glass breaking, etc.
24. Distant bell
25. Organ music
26. Chimes of midnight
   Bell (as in 24)
28. Carriage arriving
30. March music
   Crowd cheering
   Cannons
32. Cannon fire, distant
38. Ship's bell
39. Horse hooves—single rider
   Horse hooves—four riders
40. Night noises—owl, wind, etc.

NEW PLAYS

★ **HONOUR by Joanna Murray-Smith.** In a series of intense confrontations, a wife, husband, lover and daughter negotiate the forces of passion, history, responsibility and honour. "HONOUR makes for surprisingly interesting viewing. Tight, crackling dialogue (usually played out in punchy verbal duels) captures characters unable to deal with emotions ... Murray-Smith effectively places her characters in situations that strip away pretense." *–Variety* "... the play's virtues are strong: a distinctive theatrical voice, passionate concerns ... HONOUR might just capture a few honors of its own." *–Time Out Magazine* [1M, 3W] ISBN: 0-8222-1683-3

★ **MR. PETERS' CONNECTIONS by Arthur Miller.** Mr. Miller describes the protagonist as existing in a dream-like state when the mind is "freed to roam from real memories to conjectures, from trivialities to tragic insights, from terror of death to glorying in one's being alive." With this memory play, the Tony Award and Pulitzer Prize-winner reaffirms his stature as the world's foremost dramatist. "... a cross between Joycean stream-of-consciousness and Strindberg's dream plays, sweetened with a dose of William Saroyan's philosophical whimsy ... CONNECTIONS is most intriguing ..." *–The NY Times* [5M, 3W] ISBN: 0-8222-1687-6

★ **THE WAITING ROOM by Lisa Loomer.** Three women from different centuries meet in a doctor's waiting room in this dark comedy about the timeless quest for beauty – and its cost. "... THE WAITING ROOM ... is a bold, risky melange of conflicting elements that is ... terrifically moving ... There's no resisting the fierce emotional pull of the play." *–The NY Times* "... one of the high points of this year's Off-Broadway season ... THE WAITING ROOM is well worth a visit." *–Back Stage* [7M, 4W, flexible casting] ISBN: 0-8222-1594-2

★ **THE OLD SETTLER by John Henry Redwood.** A sweet-natured comedy about two church-going sisters in 1943 Harlem and the handsome young man who rents a room in their apartment. "For all of its decent sentiments, THE OLD SETTLER avoids sentimentality. It has the authenticity and lack of pretense of an Early American sampler." *–The NY Times* "We've had some fine plays Off-Broadway this season, and this is one of the best." *–The NY Post* [1M, 3W] ISBN: 0-8-222-1642-6

★ **THE LAST TRAIN TO NIBROC by Arlene Hutton.** In 1940 two young strangers share a seat on a train bound east only to find their paths will cross again. "All aboard. LAST TRAIN TO NIBROC is a sweetly told little chamber romance." *–Show Business* "... [a] gently charming little play, reminiscent of Thorton Wilder in its look at rustic Americans who are to be treasured for their simplicity and directness ..." *–Associated Press* "The old formula of boy wins girl, boy loses girl, boy wins girl still works ... [a] well-made play that perfectly captures a slice of small-town-life-gone-by." *–Back Stage* [1M, 1W] ISBN: 0-8222-1753-8

★ **OVER THE RIVER AND THROUGH THE WOODS by Joe DiPietro.** Nick sees both sets of his grandparents every Sunday for dinner. This is routine until he has to tell them that he's been offered a dream job in Seattle. The news doesn't sit so well. "A hilarious family comedy that is even funnier than his long running musical revue *I Love You, You're Perfect, Now Change.*" *–Back Stage* "Loaded with laughs every step of the way." *–Star-Ledger* [3M, 3W] ISBN: 0-8222-1712-0

★ **SIDE MAN by Warren Leight.** 1999 Tony Award winner. This is the story of a broken family and the decline of jazz as popular entertainment. "... a tender, deeply personal memory play about the turmoil in the family of a jazz musician as his career crumbles at the dawn of the age of rock-and-roll ..." *–The NY Times* "[SIDE MAN] is an elegy for two things – a lost world and a lost love. When the two notes sound together in harmony, it is moving and graceful ..." *–The NY Daily News* "An atmospheric memory play...with crisp dialogue and clearly drawn characters ... reflects the passing of an era with persuasive insight ... The joy and despair of the musicians is skillfully illustrated." *–Variety* [5M, 3W] ISBN: 0-8222-1721-X

DRAMATISTS PLAY SERVICE, INC.
440 Park Avenue South, New York, NY 10016 212-683-8960 Fax 212-213-1539
postmaster@dramatists.com www.dramatists.com

NEW PLAYS

★ **CLOSER by Patrick Marber.** Winner of the 1998 Olivier Award for Best Play and the 1999 New York Drama Critics Circle Award for Best Foreign Play. Four lives intertwine over the course of four and a half years in this densely plotted, stinging look at modern love and betrayal. "CLOSER is a sad, savvy, often funny play that casts a steely, unblinking gaze at the world of relationships and lets you come to your own conclusions ... CLOSER does not merely hold your attention; it burrows into you." *–New York Magazine* "A powerful, darkly funny play about the cosmic collision between the sun of love and the comet of desire." *–Newsweek Magazine* [2M, 2W] ISBN: 0-8222-1722-8

★ **THE MOST FABULOUS STORY EVER TOLD by Paul Rudnick.** A stage manager, headset and prompt book at hand, brings the house lights to half, then dark, and cues the creation of the world. Throughout the play, she's in control of everything. In other words, she's either God, or she thinks she is. "Line by line, Mr. Rudnick may be the funniest writer for the stage in the United States today ... One-liners, epigrams, withering put-downs and flashing repartee: These are the candles that Mr. Rudnick lights instead of cursing the darkness ... a testament to the virtues of laughing ... and in laughter, there is something like the memory of Eden." *–The NY Times* "Funny it is ... consistently, rapaciously, deliriously ... easily the funniest play in town." *–Variety* [4M, 5W] ISBN: 0-8222-1720-1

★ **A DOLL'S HOUSE by Henrik Ibsen, adapted by Frank McGuinness.** Winner of the 1997 Tony Award for Best Revival. "New, raw, gut-twisting and gripping. Easily the hottest drama this season." *–USA Today* "Bold, brilliant and alive." *–The Wall Street Journal* "A thunderclap of an evening that takes your breath away." *–Time Magazine* [4M, 4W, 2 boys] ISBN: 0-8222-1636-1

★ **THE HERBAL BED by Peter Whelan.** The play is based on actual events which occurred in Stratford-upon-Avon in the summer of 1613, when William Shakespeare's elder daughter was publicly accused of having a sexual liaison with a married neighbor and family friend. "In his probing new play, THE HERBAL BED ... Peter Whelan muses about a sidelong event in the life of Shakespeare's family and creates a finely textured tapestry of love and lies in the early 17th-century Stratford." *–The NY Times* "It is a first rate drama with interesting moral issues of truth and expediency." *–The NY Post* [5M, 3W] ISBN: 0-8222-1675-2

★ **SNAKEBIT by David Marshall Grant.** A study of modern friendship when put to the test. "... a rather smart and absorbing evening of water-cooler theater, the intimate sort of Off-Broadway experience that has you picking apart the recognizable characters long after the curtain calls." *– The NY Times* "Off-Broadway keeps on presenting us with compelling reasons for going to the theater. The latest is SNAKEBIT, David Marshall Grant's smart new comic drama about being thirtysomething and losing one's way in life." *–The NY Daily News* [3M, 1W] ISBN: 0-8222-1724-4

★ **A QUESTION OF MERCY by David Rabe.** The Obie Award-winning playwright probes the sensitive and controversial issue of doctor-assisted suicide in the age of AIDS in this poignant drama. "There are many devastating ironies in Mr. Rabe's beautifully considered, piercingly clear-eyed work ..." *–The NY Times* "With unsettling candor and disturbing insight, the play arouses pity and understanding of a troubling subject ... Rabe's provocative tale is an affirmation of dignity that rings clear and true." *–Variety* [6M, 1W] ISBN: 0-8222-1643-4

★ **DIMLY PERCEIVED THREATS TO THE SYSTEM by Jon Klein.** Reality and fantasy overlap with hilarious results as this unforgettable family attempts to survive the nineties. "Here's a play whose point about fractured families goes to the heart, mind – and ears." *–The Washington Post* "... an end-of-the-millennium comedy about a family on the verge of a nervous breakdown ... Trenchant and hilarious ..." *–The Baltimore Sun* [2M, 4W] ISBN: 0-8222-1677-9

DRAMATISTS PLAY SERVICE, INC.
440 Park Avenue South, New York, NY 10016 212-683-8960 Fax 212-213-1539
postmaster@dramatists.com   www.dramatists.com

NEW PLAYS

★ **AS BEES IN HONEY DROWN by Douglas Carter Beane.** Winner of the John Gassner Playwriting Award. A hot young novelist finds the subject of his new screenplay in a New York socialite who leads him into the world of *Auntie Mame* and *Breakfast at Tiffany's*, before she takes him for a ride. "A delicious soufflé of a satire … [an] extremely entertaining fable for an age that always chooses image over substance." –*The NY Times* "… A witty assessment of one of the most active and relentless industries in a consumer society … the creation of 'hot' young things, which the media have learned to mass produce with efficiency and zeal." –*The NY Daily News* [3M, 3W, flexible casting] ISBN: 0-8222-1651-5

★ **STUPID KIDS by John C. Russell.** In rapid, highly stylized scenes, the story follows four high-school students as they make their way from first through eighth period and beyond, struggling with the fears, frustrations, and longings peculiar to youth. "In STUPID KIDS … playwright John C. Russell gets the opera of adolescence to a T … The stylized teenspeak of STUPID KIDS … suggests that Mr. Russell may have hidden a tape recorder under a desk in study hall somewhere and then scoured the tapes for good quotations … it is the kids' insular, ceaselessly churning world, a pre-adult world of Doritos and libidos, that the playwright seeks to lay bare." –*The NY Times* "STUPID KIDS [is] a sharp-edged … whoosh of teen angst and conformity anguish. It is also very funny." –*NY Newsday* [2M, 2W] ISBN: 0-8222-1698-1

★ **COLLECTED STORIES by Donald Margulies.** From Obie Award-winner Donald Margulies comes a provocative analysis of a student-teacher relationship that turns sour when the protégé becomes a rival. "With his fine ear for detail, Margulies creates an authentic, insular world, and he gives equal weight to the opposing viewpoints of two formidable characters." –*The LA Times* "This is probably Margulies' best play to date …" –*The NY Post* "… always fluid and lively, the play is thick with ideas, like a stock-pot of good stew." –*The Village Voice* [2W] ISBN: 0-8222-1640-X

★ **FREEDOMLAND by Amy Freed.** An overdue showdown between a son and his father sets off fireworks that illuminate the neurosis, rage and anxiety of one family – and of America at the turn of the millennium. "FREEDOMLAND's more obvious links are to *Buried Child* and *Bosoms and Neglect*. Freed, like Guare, is an inspired wordsmith with a gift for surreal touches in situations grounded in familiar and real territory." –*Curtain Up* [3M, 4W] ISBN: 0-8222-1719-8

★ **STOP KISS by Diana Son.** A poignant and funny play about the ways, both sudden and slow, that lives can change irrevocably. "There's so much that is vital and exciting about STOP KISS … you want to embrace this young author and cheer her onto other works … the writing on display here is funny and credible … you also will be charmed by its heartfelt characters and up-to-the-minute humor." –*The NY Daily News* "… irresistibly exciting … a sweet, sad, and enchantingly sincere play." –*The NY Times* [3M, 3W] ISBN: 0-8222-1731-7

★ **THREE DAYS OF RAIN by Richard Greenberg.** The sins of fathers and mothers make for a bittersweet elegy in this poignant and revealing drama. "… a work so perfectly judged it heralds the arrival of a major playwright … Greenberg is extraordinary." –*The NY Daily News* "Greenberg's play is filled with graceful passages that are by turns melancholy, harrowing, and often, quite funny." –*Variety* [2M, 1W] ISBN: 0-8222-1676-0

★ **THE WEIR by Conor McPherson.** In a bar in rural Ireland, the local men swap spooky stories in an attempt to impress a young woman from Dublin who recently moved into a nearby "haunted" house. However, the tables are soon turned when she spins a yarn of her own. "You shed all sense of time at this beautiful and devious new play." –*The NY Times* "Sheer theatrical magic. I have rarely been so convinced that I have just seen a modern classic. Tremendous." –*The London Daily Telegraph* [4M, 1W] ISBN: 0-8222-1706-6

DRAMATISTS PLAY SERVICE, INC.
440 Park Avenue South, New York, NY 10016 212-683-8960 Fax 212-213-1539
postmaster@dramatists.com www.dramatists.com